Ride the Tortoise

Ride the Tortoise

Short stories by

Liesl Jobson

Published by Jacana Media (Pty) Ltd in 2013

10 Orange Street
Sunnyside
Auckland Park 2092
South Africa
(+27 11) 628-3200
www.jacana.co.za

ISBN 978-1-4314-0566-4

Edited by Helen Moffett
Cover design by publicide
Set in Cochin 10.5/14pt
Printed and bound by Ultra Litho (Pty) Ltd, Johannesburg
Job no. 001850

See a complete list of Jacana titles at www.jacana.co.za

For Brigitte,
whose listening enabled the telling

Contents

The Edge
of the Pot

THE THIN WOMAN with a baby tied on her back is the chicken-seller who usually sits outside the Lucky Dip Spaza. She jiggles against the charge office counter, calming her baby, who is just visible above a checked blanket. As if it has sobbed for a long time, it sighs, shuddering. The woman has the slanted eyes and light complexion of the Tswana people. Inspector Msomi ignores her because she did not greet him in Zulu.

If she'd noticed the scarification on his face that bespoke his tribal ancestry, or if she'd read his name, she'd have known to say "Sawubona" instead of "Dumelang". Msomi is a Zulu name. Even I know that. Maybe she can't read. She'd have done better to call him Captain. Msomi likes "an honest mistake", or so he once told me.

The Inspector says, "Uphi uDubazana, ntombi?" *Where is Dubazana, girl?* He is trying to provoke me by calling me "ntombi". He wants me to ask him to call me "Constable" or "Constable Niemandt". When I don't respond, he scowls at the empty space beside Sergeant Lebo Dubazana's name in the register. On the previous page, Lebo's signature is a vacillating zigzag, as if unsure where it belongs. The others on our shift are all here. My partner is an hour late.

"Angazi, Inspector," I say, through a drawing pin I'm holding between my lips. *I don't know.* The poem on the notice board swings at an odd angle. Beside it is a grainy wanted poster of an escaped prisoner, a suspect for the

1

rape and murder of a ten-year-old girl. I straighten and re-pin the poem, a gift from Inspector Phiri before he was found hanging in the veld.

"Awusazi?" he asks. *You don't know?* My palms sweat. I feel like I'm sucking on a sock. Ever since Phiri's funeral, I've been looking at my colleagues' faces and wondering who will go next. I look over at the baby, hoping this isn't another rape. Msomi waves at the woman to sit down on the cracked plastic chair. She perches on its edge, but the baby is restless. She stands again, swaying to settle it.

Msomi's irritation is a wasp that hasn't quite decided what to sting. Squinting over his spectacles, he wants to believe that I know where Lebo is. I don't. Nobody here does. The woman sings to her child, a haunting lullaby with vowels that twist and yearn, consonants dark.

"uDubazana uyagula?" asks Msomi. *Is Dubazana ill?* I shrug. "Phone the sick office," he says.

While I wait for the call to be answered, the baby's whimpering rises. The only other female officer on duty went to buy Msomi's cigarettes. If the woman is here to report a baby rape, Msomi will insist that I inspect the baby before accompanying the mother and child to the District Surgeon. A tiny yellow-and-black Chiefs cap peeks out of the blanket. It might be a boy. Lucky baby. Male infants are just about never raped.

A tinny voice on the phone confirms that Dubazana has not reported in sick. I move to assist the chicken-seller. Msomi blocks me, scrutinising me. He spins the vehicle logbook across the desk, jerking his thumb at it. "Reconcile the odo readings, Constable." Is this more important than the woman and her child? He rubs his hand across his chin slowly, challenging me. I open the logbook.

"Perhaps your friend is babalaas on this fine Monday morning, eh Constable?" His tone is sneering. He thinks

I'm screwing my beat partner. That thought has crossed my mind, but Lebo is married. What if he sleeps around? What if he's got Aids? That question doesn't stop the strangeness in my belly after a rough call. I still find myself wanting Lebo to hold me. When I feel that primitive urge beyond intelligence or education, I try to think Christian thoughts, but a much older religion pulses beneath my skin.

It happened first that time we found the small girl among the reeds growing below the highway. A missing child had been reported, last seen in Diepkloof Zone 3, near the Shell garage on Koma Road. The owner of the Jealous Down spaza said the girl paid for her mother's snuff with a new five-rand coin. She'd showed him the unusually coloured coin, saying, "See, Malumi, silver and gold together." Then she left for home. She'd have passed the garage to cross the busy road, but the petrol attendants never saw her return. They knew her; they used to give her bubble gum and laugh at the perfect pink bubbles she blew with her baby-doll lips. Or so they said.

Lebo and I found a sandal first, spotting it simul-taneously, and then he found the other one under a bush. It had Velcro fasteners for little fingers that couldn't yet manage buckles. Then I found a small pink sweater with a lime-green dinosaur stitched on the front. Its one remaining eye was a surprised button, snagged on an acacia. I pulled on rubber gloves and placed the sweater in a plastic Ziploc bag. Matching green leggings and a vest with a ragged lace trim had been tossed aside. Her white cotton panties had muddy footprints on them.

Lebo jogged back to radio our find to the station while I noted locations in my pocket book. A fly settled on my lip. I swatted it away and clambered down to the reeds.

When I found her head, with its row of braids ending in rainbow beads, her eyes were still open. They stared, disappointed with me for arriving so late. I staggered backwards, dropping the plastic bag. Then I spotted her naked torso a few metres away, caked in mud and blood. Her genitals had been cut out. A cloud of flies buzzed over the slashed flesh. I emptied my stomach violently before collapsing in a foetal ball.

Lebo's footsteps came towards me as he brushed through the bushes, then he was kneeling behind me, encircling me in his arms. "Sh-sh-sh. Thula, sisi, thula," he whispered, *Quiet, sister, quiet*, rocking me as I keened. He stroked my head, brushing away a strand of hair that had escaped my ponytail and was sticking in the vomit on my chin. "Be strong, Jessie. Be strong." He held my head against his chest. His nameplate was cold against my cheek. My tears subsided, but a bewildering hunger arose below my gut. "Why?" I asked. "Why?"

That was how Inspector Msomi found us. Lebo pulled me up abruptly and brushed the muddy earth from my knees.

Msomi passes behind me, bumping me. Seated right up against the desk, I can't move out his way. I pat the logbook, odometer readings tallying with the vehicles. He reads over my shoulder, his breath sour. Grape gum and Camels. I am pinned against the chair, unable to get up as he leans over me to countersign the logbook. Msomi turns at last to the woman at the counter, now bobbing anxiously to calm her screaming child. She has been waiting for twenty minutes. "Yebo?" he says, slouching over the counter toward her. *Yes?* It is a perfunctory acknowledgment.

She places two papers on the counter, child support documentation, it looks like. They've been folded so often that a brown mark now smears the crease. She whispers her request for a certified copy. Msomi bangs the stamp on the copy and signs it off without comparing it to the original. I can barely contain my relief as she shuffles out.

"Was Lebo at Emancipation last night?" I ask one of the other uniforms, a regular at the illegal shebeen behind the barracks. He wasn't.

"That dunderhead. I'll default him if he's gone AWOL," says Msomi.

Before Phiri's suicide, Constable Moshoeshoe went missing one Friday night. We'd knocked off early to celebrate payday. We sat around the green swimming pool, smoking outside the Mess Hall at the Diepkloof barracks, warmed by the flames of a braai fire. A stainless-steel urn had been unplugged and filled with ice. Beer and Jack Daniels bottles were wedged between the grey-white chunks. The plug from the urn trailed in the sand.

Moshoeshoe sat apart, guzzling whiskey from a chipped coffee mug. He'd been tipped off that a neighbour was comforting his wife while he was at work. As it so happened, Mrs Moshoeshoe had her own spies, who reported that her husband's police car stopped outside the schoolmistress' home for long periods each afternoon. The schoolmistress conducted the Sunday School choir. Was her husband undertaking criminal investigations or learning to sing on a regular basis?

As the evening wore on, Moshoeshoe got vrot. Late that night, he tipped the melted ice water from the urn into the swimming pool, then embraced it, singing, "You're as cold as ice." Lebo steered him back to the fire. The urn would never work properly again. Weaving unsteadily towards his car, Moshoeshoe threatened to "discipline" his wife. Lebo urged him to sleep it off at the barracks, but he left.

After his departure, the gossips smoking in the courtyard beside the defunct water feature said he was telling only half the story. Someone said his wife refused to sleep with him because he brought home "Omo".

"Washing powder?" I asked, woozy from two beers. But sober in daylight, nothing makes sense in Soweto. Even after two years here, I'm always playing catch-up.

"Not washing powder," said Lebo looking away, "*that disease… you know…*"

"Eish!" I said.

Why the euphemism? Nobody talks straightforwardly about Aids. Especially not at funerals – when we gather to bury a young mother or father, nobody mentions the A-word. The colleagues we've buried "got sick". In just a few weeks, they were "late". The first time I heard the word used like that, I thought someone was behind schedule and would soon turn up. It was my comprehension that was slow to arrive.

Moshoeshoe has never been found, either dead or alive. At least the press didn't get hold of the story. His vehicle is still missing; his service pistol gone too. For six months after he disappeared, Inspector Msomi wrote AWOL beside his name. At first he wrote it in large red capitals that sprawled over the lines. "AmaSotho, bayamalingara. Baya mampara." *All Sotho are malingerers and bumpkins.*

He took pleasure in scratching the angry letters in the empty space where the absent constable's signature belonged. "Unreliable and lazy, every one of them."

But when Moshoeshoe's wife and girlfriend both turned up, claiming they hadn't seen or heard from him in a week, Msomi's "AWOL" diminished until it fit between the lines. When the commander instructed him to file a missing persons report he left it to me to phone the hospitals in the city and the morgues further afield. Later I checked for vehicles exiting at the border posts. His car was still in the country. Somewhere. Every few months, I'd go through the firearm register. Nothing.

Sometimes my body betrays me when I'm with Lebo, like after that high-speed car chase. On a night raid with the Anti-Hijacking Task Team, we pulled up at a house in Tshiawelo with our headlights turned off. Detectives in unmarked sedans led us to the house on the moonless night. An officer banged on the door. Dogs barked.

"Vula isivalo! Amaphoyis' akhona!" he shouted. *Open the door for the police.*

Getting out the van, off-balance in the heavy bulletproof vest, I moved slowly. A shot hissed into the night, close enough to feel the displaced air. I dropped instinctively. Lebo went down hard next to the van. He lay on the ground, breathing heavily – a good sign. If he'd been hit, he'd be groaning. A cop behind a tree shouted that the suspect had escaped through the back yard. Men scrambled through the maze of houses.

Lebo jumped up and levered himself into the vehicle, pulled me in, and took off down to the bridge. We hurtled around corners, tyres screeching. Momentum flung me against him. If we hit a pothole, the vehicle would roll. In the next straight stretch, I reached for the seat belt I'd been drilled into wearing since infancy. There were none. I braced against the dashboard, my thigh bumping against Lebo's.

The radio crackled, ordered us back. Another team had apprehended the suspect. Chase over.

Driving back to the barracks, adrenaline still churning, my limbs too long, an intense heat started between my legs. I wanted to relax, thought of suggesting to Lebo that we go for a walk. Walk? Where? My puritanical anxiety won. I gave him a quick, chaste hug and got out the van fast. When I undressed later, my panties were moist. I recalled the smell of him, and blushed at my need.

By 9am, I've filed the vehicle log with the fuel chits stapled to its cover. Lebo doesn't seem the suicidal type. Then again, neither did Phiri. Lebo often arrives at work suffused in the fumes of Slim Lizzie's home-brew from the night before. Hands trembling, he signs in without fail. Never missed a day. His conviction rate is high. He's one of the few officers I actually trust. I've never seen him take a bribe.

When not at the tavern, he's fixing something – a broken radio, a mate's car, or a second-hand microwave. Always "a bargain". But the rubbish he collects costs more in parts and time than he can sell them for. Maybe that's why he always needs a mid-month loan.

My cell phone rings. Lebo is barely audible.

"Hey, Jess…"

"Lebo! Where are you?" It's a public phone, a terrible line.

"Sun City, babe."

"Are you crazy?" I say, thinking of the casino. "Get your butt over here. You're so deep in the soup." Surely he's not a gambler. I'm such a poor judge of character. Is he in debt too?

"Jess, can you loan me…"

His wife plays fafi on the pavement near their house, betting when he dreamed of cockerels or the moon. But the casino? It seemed unlikely.

"Get serious, Lebo, where the hell are you?"

"Sun City, sisi. Jail." The other name for the Johannesburg Prison. What's he in for? "I'm sorry to ask," he hesitated, "but I need…" The line crackles; I can't hear.

Inspector Msomi appears, and holds out his hand, wanting the phone. My phone. I can hardly refuse. I tell Lebo that the inspector wants to talk to him, and hand it over. He switches to Zulu, speaking too fast for me to follow. Imali comes up a lot. I know that one – money. Also umlungu. Whitey. That would be me.

If I'm reading this right, there's a negotiation underway about my bailing him out. Because I'm the only one in the unit who never asks for a mid-month loan? I'm also the only one without a garnishee order on my salary. Or because I'm the only one with a legitimate private job?

The others have private jobs that nobody mentions. They double as bouncers at nightclubs, bodyguards for the soccer bosses. I did a TEFL course and teach English to Chinese housewives. We all need the extra cash. I'm saving for a car. Lebo promised to find me a decent second-hand one.

"Well, Constable, maybe you can help your…" Msomi pauses before saying, "friend" as he hands me back my cell phone.

"What's he booked for?"

"Failure to pay child support."

"Which wife is after him now?"

"Both. And the girlfriend."

Girlfriend? I didn't know. I can't stop my rising colour.

"I have a little in savings," I volunteer, swallowing hard, knowing it won't come back. "I'll have to go the bank." Lebo's mates will pop out a small donation for their drinking buddy. The commander will loan him the rest. According to regulations, a senior officer is not supposed to request a loan from a junior. It is not the moment to remind Msomi.

"Inspector, what's going on with Lebo?"

"Ungazitholi usungene emhluzini ubila kanye nawo." *Don't sit at the edge of the pot, you don't want to drop into the soup.* "Be careful, Jessie," he says, leaning too close again as we queue at the automated teller machine outside the bank. I don't like it when he uses my first name. A fleck of spittle lands on my cheek. I want to wipe it off, but if I do he will apologise and wipe my face himself.

I step backwards, but stand on the woman behind me. She mutters softly.

"Sorry, ma'am," I say.

"Askies, Mama, uxolo," says Msomi, adding his apology.

He touches the sleeve as we make for the exit, dodging slow shoppers on the uneven floor. Workmen are chiselling at cracked tiles. The noise is staggering, but Msomi has his "friendly advice" face on. I lean in to hear him. "You remember Inspector Phiri?" A prickle starts behind my knees.

The inspector used to play the pennywhistle with slim fingers. A gentleman who always watered the potted plants, he'd make us scalding coffee with condensed milk and a tot of brandy on winter nights. He wrote letters to the editor of *The Sun* complaining about their shoddy journalism. He always asked me to check his spelling. When I tactfully explained how the verb of a sentence had to agree with its subject in number and person, he was delighted.

"You're a teacher, Jessie," he would say, "a real teacher."

Inspector Phiri entered *The Sun's* annual poetry contest a month before his death. The prize was a week-long holiday at a game farm, worth more than his monthly salary. He sent in a rhyming verse in beautiful penmanship. I helped him with the scansion and told him it was soulful. He smiled broadly that day and gave me the afternoon off.

"Ja, Inspector Msomi, I remember Phiri," I say. I wish I'd understood his last gift to me. The paper on which his poem was written has turned brittle on the office noticeboard. Could I have seen the warning signs?

"You know why he hanged himself?"

I don't. The verse gave no clues either. I climb into the passenger seat and say, "Stress?"

Msomi's eyebrows twitch, as if to say, "Guess again." Where is this going? He turns the key.

"What's this got to do with Lebo?" I ask, bewildered.

"uPhiri uwele esobweni." *Phiri fell in the soup.* He sounds self-righteous.

"You mean…" I fumble for words, trying to grasp the meaning, unsure whether to respond with disapproval or pity. What's the subtext? "He did something wrong?"

"He was under investigation, Jessie." Msomi holds my gaze with a knowing look. "For corruption." His gold-capped tooth sparkles in the sunlight before he shifts the gear into reverse.

"So?"

"He had Nigerian connections…"

Phiri? I can't imagine him doing anything irregular. I frown.

"You don't believe?" asks Msomi, shoving the gear into first and pulling off. The vehicle judders under a ropy clutch.

"I don't know."

"I'm telling you."

Msomi is telling me something else too, but I can't decode. "Please explain, Inspector?"

He clicks his tongue, looking about furtively even though we're alone in the van. He whispers, "You always have money, Jess. People are jealous…"

"I teach English to foreigners, Inspector. You know that."

"If one day you discover you are unable to help somebody out, somebody who needs your assistance, for example, *you* could find yourself under investigation."

My jaw drops. "Lebo's my buddy. Of course I'll help him."

The inspector rests his hand on my thigh. My stomach lurches.

"Choose your friends carefully, Constable."

I want to push his hand away, but move my knees together discreetly instead.

"Just a fatherly tip," he says, grinning like my father never had.

Am I supposed to be grateful? The pressure of his leg against mine increases. I can't think.

"But I have permission from the Station Commissioner, Inspector, *written* permission. You've seen it."

I tell myself I'm imagining his advances. He doesn't like me; my scrawny body is not his type. He likes voluptuousness, the "Number Seven, straight from heaven" girls that flock to the police van when we are out together; women with huge bosoms and solid buttocks. I'm a "Number Two, Maseru", too stringy by far.

Maybe his hand on my leg is just friendliness. They say Zulus are more open, less inhibited. I want to dismiss my anxiety as paranoia.

"I teach after hours. It doesn't interfere with my duties." My voice is too shrill.

"I understand, Constable, but everyone knows the Chinese…"

Mrs Tsuen has an elaborate embroidered dragon guarding the entrance to her facebrick Cyrildene home. Each Tuesday evening I place my large black boots beside her dainty sequined slippers, small as a child's. In her country, the dragon brings power. And good luck. I follow her to the dining-room table with footsteps that are inaudible in my blue wool socks. Even though I tower above her, she leads me by the arm and I am ten again, visiting a friend's home, a safe house, where people speak in low voices and bad things never happen.

"Everyone knows," says Msomi, the sensation on my skin becoming unbearable, "that they are drug traffickers."

"That's quite a generalisation, Inspector," I say, risking his disapproval. He dislikes opposition, especially from women, white women most of all. He'll dismiss my opinion, maybe start ranting. On previous occasions he's told me I think myself a "clever", a "learned somebody", hastening to explain that I'm really a know-nothing idiot. Today, he is oddly silent.

A polished brass Buddha rests on Mrs Tsuen's mantelpiece. In last week's lesson, we covered the terminology of art: sculpture, figure, painting, form. Afterwards, she served noodles fragrant with lemongrass and sesame oil. She plucked generous portions from the dish with chopsticks and arranged them in delicate bowls. While I eat, fumbling with the chopsticks, she sips green tea and speaks with fluttering hands. I admire the cerise-tongued orchids blooming extravagantly on her front porch, creamy blossoms emerging and unfurling week by week. Tonight we'll glean the vocabulary of plants: soil, stem, stamen. Open. Bud. Tonight we'll uncover the mysteries of metaphor.

The Inspector's hand returns to the steering wheel as he veers sharply across two lanes. "Just be careful, ntombi. If that private work you do is not strictly legal, you better watch the edge of the pot…"

Mrs Tsuen's diminutive husband nods deferentially when he returns from work. He sloughs off his plain leather slip-ons, looking tired in his old-fashioned suit. A key player in the Triads? An abalone smuggler? Hard to imagine.

His muted stoop, however, is familiar. Mr Tsuen shuffles like my father did after long hours of balancing books and years of tedium. If he ever picks up a firearm, he will not point it at a double-dealing gangster. He will aim it, like my father, at the roof of his mouth.

"I'll watch my step, Inspector."

An advertisement appeared in *The Workplace* this morning. I cut it out and folded it up. English teachers are wanted in Dubai. If you teach overseas for a few years, I've heard, you can save enough to buy a house. I could go and teach in a palace.

"Make sure you do. People are not the same," he says.

Stopping outside the station, he doesn't immediately open the door. His hand returns to my leg. I hand him the money, crisp notes smelling still of ink. He folds them with an air of satisfaction, as if I were no longer there. I want to ask when Lebo will be back; want to ask his girlfriend's name. I want to know if she's also a "'Number Two, Maseru".

Msomi strikes up before getting out, filling the cab with smoke. I wave it away, my eyes burning, and hs scowl turns into a smirk. He walks to the cinder-block offices with a longer stride. He looks taller. The chicken-seller from the Lucky Dip Spaza sees him, cowers. Her baby is still crying.

My shift is over. I reach for my pen and pocket book. Time to sign out for the day. The article from *The Workplace* falls out from between the pages. English teachers are also needed in Beijing.

When Mrs Tsuen makes duck soup, she serves it with short-handled spoons. Flat and shallow. Made from porcelain.

Just three lines remain on the right-hand page of my pocket book. Msomi likes me to leave a lot of space for him to countersign. Complains if I cramp his style. I turn the page, but this afternoon, instead of writing the time and my force number, I draw a dragon.

Still Life in the Art Room

DALILA PACES ABOUT the art room like a plover, with jerky steps. When she stops moving, her head is cocked, as if listening to some half-heard thing.

"Mafudu is restless today," says Sikelela, an eleventh grader, under his breath. He rinses a sable brush in a jar of water.

"Mafudu indeed!" The scissors grumble on the shelf. "Why don't these children call their teacher 'ma'am'?"

"She's probably dieting," says a girl.

"These children show no respect," murmurs a charcoal drawing-stick.

"Go awaaay!" cries a loerie in the tree outside the classroom, startling Dalila.

"Silence," she says.

Shortly after her return from compassionate leave nearly a year ago, Sikelela had noticed the scraps of paper filled with tortoises on the teacher's desk. Dalila had passed the time doodling serried ranks of the ancient creatures marching eastward toward an imaginary shoreline beyond the page.

"You really like tortoises, Ma'am?"

"Mmm," she'd nodded, flipping the pad closed.

Dalila did not point out that what she drew were turtles, not tortoises. No Zulu word exists for the former, only an extension that approximates: ufudu-lwaso-lwandle or the tortoise-of-the-water. The nickname Mafudu stuck. Miss Tortoise.

Dalila had been unperturbed by the nickname. She recognised that it fit her heavy tread and fixed gaze, but had no desire to change either. She was relieved that her students had noticed only her eccentric drawings. They hadn't heard, it seemed, the rattling palette boxes in the cabinet or the shuffling of the sketch boards. Perhaps these sounds were lost against the scraping chairs and the grinding of the old-fashioned pencil sharpener on her desk. A few days before Sikelela's observation, she'd presented an easy lesson, saying, "Today we're doing 'Take-a-line-for-a-walk'. Who knows which artists developed this style?" She nodded towards the girl with unruly dreads whose hand was raised while the question was being asked.

"Klee, Ma'am," said Refiloe.

"Yes. Another artist?"

"Miro," answered Salmaan.

Dalila switched on the overhead projector to demonstrate. "This way you let an abstract line take shape, as it curves, zigzags, makes corners; let it wander freely over the page." Her hand whizzed over the screen. "Now shift the page until you see something recognisable." She swivelled the transparency around. "Maybe you'll see an eye or a claw. Look, here I've got the skeleton of a tree." She pointed with one hand. With the other, she made rapid gestures filling in leaves like eyelashes, twigs like feathery bones and beaks. "Keep going until the whole page is covered in detail." It was the last time her hand moved swiftly, unselfconsciously for many months.

"The other way of performing this task requires some planning to create a specific image. It is more controlled and presents a bigger challenge." She put another transparency on the projector and drew the tail of a turtle, raised the hump, formed the head, the flippers and lower carapace. Without lifting her pen, she entered the shell cavity, interweaving three rows of scales. Lastly, she created a diminishing spiral in the head cavity to form the eye out of negative white space.

"Try a waterfall, a skyline, or a garden. Whatever you do, keep your pen on the paper."

The class had already begun while she talked. The exercise was a favourite. She switched off the projector and drew another turtle, this one on a piece of paper, and then another beside it before returning to check her students' progress. She stopped a boy about to erase his work, "Keep going," she said over his shoulder. Pointing to an empty space on his page she said, "Keep it loose and free; don't think too hard."

The bell rang. The students gathered their books and pencils and sauntered out. Once they'd gone, Dalila completed an entire sheet of inch-long turtles. She put the page in the bottom drawer of her desk, the first page of identical scribbles that would accumulate over a year. Soon hundreds of miniature beasts were crammed into her desk, scraping their flippers, yearning for release. An erratic fluttering sound, barely audible, caught her attention. It sounded like the overhead projector's fan slowing after being switched off. But it was under its cover, unused, in the storeroom. She opened the drawer. The noise stopped.

Today is the first anniversary of her mother's passing.

"No cartoons today," hisses a flat pencil.

"Draw us a turtle, Mafudu," taunts a coloured pencil.

Dalila drums her fingers on her desk fifteen minutes before the final bell of the day. She chivvies the daydreaming Refiloe and complains at Salmaan's dithering. Ten minutes early she says, "Finish up. Don't start another colour. Put

17

your folios away." The students look up. Surprised, they comply.

As the last one leaves, Dalila flips over an empty bucket placing it upside down, in front of the window. The label stuck to the bottom reads Powder Tempera: light green. The colour of hospital walls. Residues of poster paint ingrained in the plastic release a faint odour of sour dust. Usually she constructs still-life compositions on a plinth in the centre of the room. Today she needs a different perspective.

She removes a faded kikoi from her tog bag and holds it to her face, inhaling deeply.

Her mother brought it back from Nairobi, a few weeks before getting ill. The open suitcase had released the fragrance of grassy plains, Kenyan shillings and Watamu Beach, where Dalila lived as a child. She had walked beside the waves holding her grandmother's hand. They found a strange depression in the sand.

"Look, a green turtle nest," said Bibi. "Turtles lay their eggs, then leave them to hatch."

"Does their mother not stay with them?" Dalila asked.

"No. The hatchlings must dash toward the surf before the gulls catch them. Only the lucky ones make it into the sea."

"They go in search of their mama and papa?" asked Dalila.

"They go to continue the cycle of life."

"Do they ever find them?"

"Turtles don't think that way, but they return here throughout their life."

"Return to Watamu?"

"The females will return to lay their eggs here when they are forty years old."

"They return looking for their parents," said the girl.

"Hmmm."

"Bibi?"

"Green turtles live to be ninety."

"Do the babies find their parents?" Dalila tugged on Bibi's skirt.

"Hmmm."

Dalila had already learned that when Bibi said, "Hmmm" in that mournful tone, she would not reply, and it served no point to ask again. There were many questions for which Bibi had no answers, including why Dalila's parents had been gone so long. Bibi didn't know where they were. Perhaps they were attending a congress in Dar es Salaam or a conference in Botswana, or were sneaking in and out of South Africa. They never told her. It was safer that way.

That night Dalila dreamed of late hatchlings, flopping in vain against the outgoing tide. They were almost at the shore when hovering gulls plucked them from the sand, their flippers swimming in midair. Dangled low over the water, the babies could see their parents. Then the gulls swooped to the beach where they cracked open the shells and gorged on the rich meat. Dalila woke sobbing.

Bibi cradled her, rocking her back to sleep, crooning, "Harambee, harambee, tuimbe pamoja. Tujenge serikali. Harambee."

She sang slowly, in the key of blackness. It sounded like a song for harvesting serpents. The next morning the news came that Dalila's father had opened a letter bomb in Lusaka.

Dalila pinches her nostrils and blows hard. Her ears pop. Her sinuses feel as if she has swum a mile underwater. She wonders if she developed an allergy to paint. The theme of today's lesson is identifying environmental and historical factors that influence visual artists.

19

Sikelela has brought a mbira, the traditional herd boy's piano. Salmaan's flag provides the backdrop and Refiloe's leggy strelitzias add colour. An exhibition of the work is planned for the Heritage Day celebration, and the president of the country is scheduled to visit the school that his grandchildren attended.

"Here we go again," sighs the bucket.

"Another plastic snake, ja?" mutters a thin yellow stripe woven into the kikoi.

"Be quiet," says Dalila, sniffing. She will not tolerate the voices today. Like her students, they pay her little attention.

"You should stick to porcelain dolls," says the bucket, "in gingham frocks and lacy petticoats."

"We haven't seen dolly for a while," says a cerise stripe.

Dalila's grandmother had sewn her party dresses, Western-style, in pastel shades, with matching dresses for the dolls from leftover fabric scraps. Peering through her bifocals, Bibi formed delicate stitches. Then she braided Dalila's hair in satin ribbons of the same shade. Dalila tried to braid her dolls' straight blonde hair, but it slipped from her fingers, refusing to hold the weave.

"Does porcelain ever come in shades of brown?"

"Hmmm," said Bibi.

Dalila drapes the kikoi, which has softened with washing, over the bucket, letting the stripes fall in a gentle curve. Once there were traces of her mother's scent in the cotton, a faint whiff of crisp herbal beer even, the brand her father had allowed her to sip when she sat on his knee that last time.

"No, Mandla," her mother had scolded. He had laughed at his daughter smacking her lips, but had whisked the bottle away.

After her father died, her mother walked along the

beach with a kikoi wrapped around her thin hips. She had always been a round, comfortable figure. She stopped eating until clothes hung on her angular form. She'd sit alone in the sand, staring at the horizon for hours. Dalila would watch her from afar. The following breeding season, a record low number of eggs were documented by Turtlewatch Kenya. Her grief scared the females away. They refused to lay.

The shushing in Dalila's ears is like waves inside a seashell. She tries to depressurise her nasal chambers again, but there is no relief. The turtles scuttle in the drawer. She places the potted plant on top of the bucket. Sunlight reflects off the finely demarcated green-and-white leaves.

Dalila had taken a slip of the hen-and-chickens plant from her mother's balcony garden when the flat was sold to cover the doctor's bills. She left the cutting in a bottle of water. When it developed roots, she transplanted it into a large ukhamba, a traditional Zulu beer pot she bought at the Rosebank market.

"Those shocking shades will quite outdo me." The pot plant glares at the bold kikoi. "My delicate stripes will be utterly lost."

"Hen lady, relax your sphincter," says the bucket.

"How uncouth," says the plant.

Dalila runs her fingers over the elaborate patterns, Iron Age motifs, incised into the dark clay. She wishes she had a banana frond to frame her composition, but Johannesburg's winter frost burns the tropical plants. There were banana groves around Gogo's kraal. Dalila recalls visiting her paternal grandmother in Gingindlovu before her father fled into exile.

Gogo showed her how to twist sticky coils of clay over bunches of rolled grass to make an ukhamba. Dalila was about six years old. Her cousin Zodwa terrified her at bedtime with stories about green mambas.

When they walked along the muddy path to the long-drop toilet, Zodwa screamed, pointing into the grass beside Dalila's feet: "Snake! Be careful!" The first time it happened, Dalila wet her pants and ran to her father. The sniggering Zodwa disappeared into the long stalks of sugar cane with the other village girls. The second time it happened, her father comforted her: "Gogo's mean stick will talk to that naughty Zodwa." Dalila was not comforted.

This morning before school as Dalila sipped her coffee, an article in *The Star* grabbed her attention:

GABORONE – The remains of Thami Mnyele were exhumed on Wednesday from Gaborone's New Stands Cemetery for reburial at home. Mnyele, a gifted graphic artist, was one of twelve ANC cadres killed by the South African Defence Force in a cross-border raid on 14 June 1985. His artwork had been deliberately destroyed in the attack. This soft-spoken gentleman, who had a passion for poetry and music, will be buried in Tembisa after a memorial service at the Mehlareng Stadium.

Dalila took the newspaper in shaking hands into her tiny garden to gather herself. On the wooden bench beside the lemon tree, she recalled her indebtedness to Thami Mnyele, the kind uncle she had met once at Beitbridge with her father.

They had just fled South Africa in a hot, gritty train, and were both tired and thirsty from the long journey. A stranger arrived with two cans of cold Coca-Cola. Her father gave her a pen and an empty envelope to keep her busy while they had an important meeting.

"Draw me a picture of Mama," he said.

Dalila drew a tiny train chugging around the edge of the envelope. In the centre was a little house. Her mother waved from its window where she had remained to cover for her husband and to sell their few belongings. Uncle Thami noticed the girl's picture, and reached into his briefcase. He brought out a pad of paper and some pencil crayons. At the time, she thought he was trying to keep her from disturbing the adults. But he had taken the drawings she offered him. He admired them, praised her, and remembered.

A few weeks later, Uncle Thami sent her her first set of paints. When the slip for the parcel had arrived bearing her name, she waited with Bibi in a long queue at the post office. When the post-office clerk eventually placed the mysterious parcel in her hands, she itched to open it right there at the counter. Bibi stopped her. The clerk gave Dalila a toffee to reward her patience.

That was when the rustling of brown paper was still sweet, when string and sealing wax meant only that one had been remembered.

A few weeks later her mother appeared unexpectedly, and Dalila tried to piece together the whispered fragments she overheard while pretending to sleep.

"Is this Mandla's child?" asked Bibi.

Dalila couldn't see in the dark whether her mother nodded or shook her head.

"Does he know?"

"He must not," said her mother.

"How often?"

"Every night for two weeks."

"And what else?"

Stifled sobs were the only answer.

"Is Mama very sick?" asked Dalila the following morning.

"Don't worry," said Bibi. "Your mother will be all right. These are old screams your mother is passing. They will go. When a woman's screams get stuck inside, her sisters have ways to set them free…"

An old woman from the village arrived with herbs and oils. She rubbed Dalila's mother's belly and pressed cool cloths against her forehead. Later she bled into the long-drop. When Dalila went to relieve herself, she stared in horror at the livery chunks that caught the sunlight through the cracked tin roof.

This morning the deep purple irises growing beneath the lemon tree reminded her of the previous winter. On her mother's last day, she'd taken a bunch of the flowers in a Heinz bottle. It was a make-do arrangement since her mother's favourite vase had been stolen in the hospital. Perhaps a nurse recognised the fine crystal that had been a wedding present.

In the ward, she had wiped her mother's face with a warm cloth and brushed her thin grey hair. Her mother whispered in the oxygen mask. Dalila couldn't hear.

"Pardon, Mama, what was that?" she asked, bending close. Her mother's rapid breath smelled fruity.

"You are my blessing," said her mother.

Dalila reached beneath the lemon tree to pick a single stem with a bud, an unfurling bloom and a fully opened flower. Back in her kitchen, she placed it in a moistened blob of cotton wool, twisting silver foil around it. A sudden yearning to paint its yellow tongue pecked at the inside of her heart. She remembered the tiny beak of a green turtle poking through the last egg at the bottom of the nest.

An angry gull had hovered overhead as it struggled free. She had chased the bird away and urged the baby on. The gull swooped and dived above. Dalila shouted at it, flapping her arms. "Hurry, little one." She faced her grandmother, crying. She wanted to pick it up, to carry it to the sea.

"If you carry that baby, it cannot develop strong flippers for swimming. It will be too weak for the ocean," said Bibi.

"But it will never get there." Dalila chased the gulls away, over and over, until the tiny turtle slipped into the waves.

Beyond the wrought-iron school gates, a queue of children waits at the bus stop. A lemon rolls off the table. Dalila catches it.

"Your roots smell off," says a stripe in the kikoi.

"Too much water," say the leaves curling over the edge of the ukhamba. Dalila blows her nose.

"School out?" asks another stripe.

"No peace unto the wicked," says the lemon.

Sikelela and Refiloe disappear into a rickety taxi headed for Soweto.

Dalila had shown her mother the striated throat of the iris. The old woman lifted a frail arm to touch its indigo petal, and then removed her oxygen mask.

"Put it against my cheek."

Dalila had neither words nor tears. No question lingered in the folds of the hospital curtains. Not a tear fell onto the pale green linen. Dalila readjusted her mother's mask.

That evening, she had tried to paint her mother's hand holding hers, but all she had to show hours later was a blank sheet of paper. That night, and every night since then, her paint box remained still silent. Nothing else let up: the chatter of desks, the prattle of chairs, the mumbling of the classroom blinds. Even the kiln in the corner sighed periodically. In her drawer, the turtles waved their flippers in agitation. But neither the pastels nor the oil paints made a murmur. The blues: phthalo, cerulean and sapphire all remained silent. Ultramarine, turquoise and Madonna blue lay like miniature coffins in her paint box. The flat and round sablette brushes lingered, soundless.

Dalila unclasps the long string of pearls her mother wore and drapes them over the lemons.

"Beats a plastic snake, I guess," says the yellow stripe.

"Pearls," says a lemon in an irritable tone. "Not very good quality."

"Hush," says Dalila. The pearls slip and clatter on the tiled floor. She picks them up and curls them around the base of a tomato-sauce bottle containing the irises.

"Why can't we be juxtaposed against a simple urn?" asks the plant, glaring at the shabby bottle. Dalila chews a hangnail and rearranges a lemon. She removes a little package wrapped in paper towel from her tog bag. She places it, unopened, beside the composition. The pearls glint in the sunlight.

Her mother had pulled the plastic mask off and said, "Take this away." Dalila tried to slip the mask back over her face, but it separated from the oxygen tube, bubbling loudly. The papery skin of her mother's cheeks was greyish against her dark-blue lips. Her mother turned away. "I don't want it any more. It's killing me."

Dalila opens the package, removes the oxygen mask and sets it beside the largest lemon. The mask, shaped like a ghoulish nostril, has a faint green tinge. She tries to identify the exact sheen: copper resinate, viridian, verdigris, cobalt green. Turning it in the light, she recalls the many-hued shells of the baby turtles.

"What next?" ask the pearls.

"Who can tell?" answers a stripe.

Very softly, the kikoi starts to hum, "Harambee, harambee…"

Dalila's ears are finally clear. The loerie in the tree outside calls, "Go awaaay."

Her mother, trying to get out of the bed, had gasped, "Take me home. I don't want to die here."

"Okay, Mama," said Dalila, cradling her. With her free arm, she pressed the button that called the nurse. She wanted to ask whether home meant Watamu Beach, or the little flat in Yeoville.

"I want to lie beside Mandla again. It's been too long."

"Shhh, Mama, shhh," she stroked her mother's hand.

"Where will you bury me?"

"Watamu," she said to soothe her mother. She still believed, even then, that she'd improve enough to be taken back to her ancestral village, but the hospital bills had precluded that.

Dalila buried her mother in the alien soil of Westpark Cemetery, which lies at the base of the Melville Koppie, under a scraggly oleander that drops toxic pink blossoms onto her grave all year long.

Dalila wipes the textured paper with a damp sponge. Her movement across the easel is swift and focused. She blends the under-wash in a palette cup with a wide hake brush, forming a streak of colour, and another. When she looks up again, the loerie is perched on a branch. Its crown fans out. The large grey bird lifts into the air and flies off. The only sound is the wind in the leaves.

Soda Lakes

SUNSCREEN, WATER BOTTLE, towel, cap, socks. A light southerly breeze catches the spoons of our blades as we carry them to the dock. The reeds growing near the slipway are swaying and the surface of the water ripples like stressed silk. We stride back to the boat shed, Jan and I, to take the trestles out. A drooping cobweb sticks to her shoulder. I reach to brush it away but stop myself, glad she doesn't notice. We line the trestles up a few metres apart, ready to receive the double scull we're going to row.

Jan's home club is on Strathclyde Loch, in Glasgow. "It's a man-made lake," she says, "built on a demolished palace and an old mining village. The water is shallow. We don't get waves like you do here."

Water without waves? Sounds odd. Later I check it out online. I do that a lot, looking up stuff I know nothing about. I discovered Jan was right on the construction details of the loch, but I found no mention of the absence of waves.

I watch rowing videos too. That's how I learned how to re-enter a shell once it's flipped. Admittedly I only looked that up after I'd fallen out and couldn't get back in. I'd tried to propel myself back up and in, but when I tried to stand, the deep mud sucked me down. With my feet gripped in the slime, my knees twisted unnaturally, the old scar tissue refusing to give. I knew better than to jerk or yank. I eased my feet back up slowly and floated myself out and over the mud, holding onto the hull, waiting for help to arrive. It was a long wait; a cold one too. The old-timers in the club

28

scolded me, said I shouldn't be rowing in the dead of winter anyway. Should never row alone. But there was nobody to go out with me. Nobody wanted to walk through the sludge where the water level had dropped. I had been desperate.

"What's the licensing protocol for rowing here?" asks Jan, a recent arrival in Cape Town. She's a microbiologist, a post-doc at the university. She is researching the soda lakes in the Great Rift Valley. When she tells me this I imagine clear and bubbling water, remembering the pools of boiling mud at the hot springs at Rotorua. As a teenager visiting New Zealand, I didn't know that water emerging from the ground could be so hot. My finger smarted for days from the burn I got when I dipped it into the water.

"Licensing protocol?" I ask. Mohammed wheels into view. He has just arrived for his training session.

"In London you need a licence to row."

"This isn't London," I say. "You go. You row. You fall out. Nobody knows." Stuff happens here. You wish it didn't. Probably happens everywhere. Doesn't even have anything to do with rowing, per se. Like that kid from Oxford, a nineteen-year-old medical student, whose parents were in Namibia. He fell out of a single canoe and broke his arm. Or rather, the sudden jolt as he steadied the boat caused the break in his arm, and *then* he fell out. This information was only pieced together later, at the hospital, once they discovered he was riddled with bone tumours. Reading about neoplastic growth tissue on Wikipedia, I ran my hands over the scars where my kneecaps once were. I read symptoms, treatment, prognosis. Some things you come back from.

"Which is our boat?" asks Jan. I point to the blue double. "Wicked," she says, "she's brand new."

"New enough."

We slide *Catalyst* off the rack, roll her riggers, hoist

her to our shoulders. We settle her on the trestles, check the footplates, runners and seats. Mohammed watches, rolling a cigarette as we carry her to the water, minding the molehills that can cause one to stumble. Mohammed emails me. I don't think he knows who I am. I think he emails everybody on the club mailing list. Or maybe just the women – I've never asked any of the others.

Jan says, "If you win a race in London, you get points on your licence." I can't imagine winning a race. Can't imagine racing, having started rowing just a year ago. I fall out a lot too, but don't tell Jan that. She might be less interested in rowing with me.

About a month ago I arrived at the jetty and there she was, talking to the club commodore, towering above him. Her light-orange hair was scraped into a tight ponytail and her thighs bulged under a black-and-white trisuit. Her knees formed sharp points. She'd come down wanting a row. I offered to go out with her in a double. Immediately I'd felt ridiculous, short as I am, and hardly knowing how to row myself.

Now Jan drills me on the water: square blades, no arms, body swing and power strokes. "Tap-down, slide. Drive and finish. Get out clean." A pelican, more snowy than pink, swoops down and settles near the reeds. I catch my breath. I want to tell her about the intimacy I disturbed the other morning, but if I tell her about pelican sex she'll think I'm weird.

"Did you hear about Andy Holmes?" she asks, but I'm a new sculler, and don't know the big names of the sport.

"No," I say, "I only know Rika, the South African who went to the Beijing Olympics." What a goddess. I love Rika. I say, "I used to go to her ergo classes. Brilliant. Now I work most evenings, so I seldom go. But what happened to Andy Holmes?"

"He was an Olympic gold medallist. Paired with Steve Redgrave. Caught Weil's disease on the Thames."

Wheels disease? I'd never heard of that. Must look it up. Do the wheels beneath the seat loosen toxins on the aluminium slide? Or is there a spinal complication caused by the wheels' motion? I ask her about it but in the bow, Jan can't hear. We're pitching into a headwind. The boat moves as we pull together. It's a 2000-metre course. Behind me, she instructs: "Steady paddle at twenty. Prepare for pyramids."

I get ready for the rate increase, slow my mind, brace my shoulders, back and down. "Next stroke, up two." The first call unleashes a rush. We're at twenty-two strokes per minute. I'm concentrating on my balance. "Next stroke, up two." Jan's fitter than me, and younger. I'm matching her pace, technique still clean. Shoulders over hips. Feet even. At the 1000-metre buoy she says, "Next stroke, up two." Not enough air. Boat wobbles. Breathe. Never pushed so hard. "Next stroke, up two." Brain-beat-heart-tight-burn-blind. Hold. Focus. Panic. God. Jan says, "Down two." A couple of strokes later she says, "Down two…" Then again, "Down two…"

We rest near the Hart Memorial shed. My breath is ragged, my heart a drum roll in my ears, slowing gradually to individual beats. How do you know if you're having a heart attack?

Would Jan want to hear about Keith Hart, who had a coronary on the water? Probably not. When Keith collapsed, the boat tipped and his partner panicked. He couldn't keep him afloat and swam to shore to raise help. They searched until sunset but, mired in the deep mud, Keith was invisible. When the police divers found him at dawn, the catfish hadn't considered his widow's finer feelings.

I drain my water bottle, then remember to ask about the disease that the British rower got. She tells me about the waterborne parasite that comes from the urine of rats. "It's mostly tropical," she says, "but seasonal in the UK. Our coach in London really drilled us about keeping open wounds covered. Boat bite and blisters is how the parasites get in. It was too sad."

"Yeah?" I ask.

"Fatal."

"Oh, fuck."

"Andy Holmes was just fifty. He had a new baby. His fifth child."

"No parasites here," I say, wanting to turn to sweeter matters, "just jacanas and herons. Oh, and the hippo at Rondevlei." But what do I know, really? There must be heaps of crap in this water. I have fallen into it about thirty times so far, and never got sick. The hippo escapes when copper thieves cut the security fence to the sewage works. But they've tagged the hippo now with a microchip for quick retrieval.

That day I fell out and got stuck in the mud was extremely strange. It was like a clump of mud fell from the sky, landed on my runner and stopped my seat dead in the tracks. My body's momentum, having just pushed off the footboard, kept me going, right off the seat, onto the tracks. I couldn't stop the boat flipping over. Hitting the water, I couldn't stop gasping. I'd fallen in often enough, but never in such cold water. Disoriented, I swam away from the sandbank where I could have stood to get back in the boat. Instead, I swam toward the closer side of the vlei, not anticipating the problem of the mud. I should have swum back to the other side, but I was too cold to think straight.

A day or so later, I read about the hippo's escape. It had happened at the same time as my escapade. My grandmother believed in water faeries, some protective, others malevolent. Undines, mermaids and selkies were slightly odd but less mean-spirited than the kelpies and sprites. My grandmother was from Scotland. Do faeries feature in Jan's imaginings? Perhaps Mami Wata, the fey folk's African counterpart, hangs out at the soda lakes.

"This is supposed to be a *fresh* water lake?" says Jan.

I point out the concrete tanks just visible over the ridge, "The sewage treatment plant washes out to sea, but when the north wind blows you wake up and smell the *E. coli*."

Jan works on my technique, telling me to feel the weight of the water on the blade at the catch. "Get a level draw through. Balance your body weight on the blade handle, then hang, as if you're suspended." Having somebody watch you and help you fix a thing right there in the boat doesn't compare with trying to figure it out from a book. I feel a rush of gratitude every time she goes out in a boat with me. Could she be a friend?

Instead of filing my tax online, I procrastinate, checking the definition of "friend". For while I am *a person attached to another by feelings of affection or personal regard*, I cannot be sure she feels the same way. Then again, she is *a person who gives assistance*, which technically makes her a friend, but a dictionary cannot read body language, cannot intuit gesture, facial expression.

Jan emails later with the technical tips and balancing exercises. There's an X before she signs off. I wonder what that means. Her PS at the end reads, "Don't try this alone." Despite the warnings, I row alone. Well, almost alone. Last week while I rested after a sprint, my oars aligned on the feather, an otter on the bank caught my eye. The little creature stopped, one paw poised in the air. Then it slipped below the surface without a splash.

Jan told me about one of the soda lakes in Kenya,

which is home to a huge population of flamingos. Every two years or so, the toxicity gets too high and they die off in enormous numbers, while the remaining birds settle at another lake. They suspect a nearby battery factory is dumping heavy metals into the water.

This year the flamingos came back to Zeekoevlei. Apparently they haven't been around for six years. When I went out on the water again, I'd forgotten that, was focused on learning to row straight. I set my stern in line with the buoy and held it there, inhaling down the slide, exhaling on the drive. With my left arm weaker than my right, my course was a zigzag of drift and correct. Watching the buoy, I'd stopped minding my course. I didn't see the flamingos on the sandbank behind me until they were a vast pink flurry, neither cawing nor cackling, but a breathy beating of a hundred wings alighting and passing overhead. I wanted to weep at their beauty; afraid they'd leave again, never to return. But before my tears could gather, the birds began their descent to the deserted beach in front of the old pump house.

"Too much politics in Kenya," says Jan.

"Not just Kenya," I say, thinking of Mohammed and the other disabled athletes who row in boats that are junk. There should be Lotto money for them, but it got "lost" on the way. Months ago they were promised a new path to the dock, to facilitate wheelchair access and help the blind guys to get down to the water, but the grass still grows in matted clumps through cracks in the old concrete.

"You can't get permits to take samples from the lake," says Jan. "Government wants it hushed up. The die-offs haven't been studied. Too damn sad." I read up on the soda lakes, learn that they're found mostly in subtropical latitudes in rain-shadow zones, that they are impermanent in nature and that their equivalent on land are soda deserts, which contain the desiccated remains of the soda lakes. I discover that tectonic activity created shallow depressions that then formed closed basins collecting ground water and the run-off from seasonal streams coming from the surrounding highlands.

Surface evaporation rates exceed the rate of inflow of water, allowing the dissolved minerals to concentrate into a caustic alkaline brine.

Last week, Jan met me early because I had to run a poetry workshop. I appreciated that. A friend is *a person who is on good terms with another.* As we went out across the small bay my catch was late; I rushed the slide. We pitched and jolted till she called, "Easy up." We drifted to a stop, me panting and jangled. I'd forgotten my water bottle on the dock. "Where are you today?" she asked. "'Cause you're not in the boat."

"I'm thinking about the writing workshop for rape survivors later today," I said. "How do you prepare for such a thing?" I suspected that was too much information already, after all, I hardly know Jan. We've only rowed together about three times, but unable to stop, I continued, "I'm supposed to encourage them to write about it. Poetry is therapeutic." I looked over my shoulder at Jan. She nodded. "Last time I ran the course, this girl in the workshop told us… she was just a kid…"

I can say no more. Even if I don't say her name, it's wrong to tell her story. But I'd flinched when she shared her ordeal, unable to conceal my shock. In the boat, six months later, I still shuddered. Jan reached forward and patted my back. We sat a while in silence. A friend is *a person who is not hostile.*

Today, again, the water is calm, our balance perfect. The riffle of bubbles bursting against the shell is a burbling whisper. As the bow breaks the surface tension our blades pop in perfect rhythm. We head back from the weir and angle up to the dock in a smooth arc. Outside the boathouse we wash off the boat. Sponge down the riggers; spray off the blades. I point out the waterline, a solid stripe from bow to stern.

"Wicked smooth," says Jan.

"Not too shabby, girls," says Bart, an old guy who has been rowing for fifty years, "but your body swing's out of sync."

"The easiest thing to spot out the boat," mutters Jan under her breath, "the hardest to fix inside it."

He notices me looking at Jan. In a voice laden with innuendo, he says, "Remember, girls, you got to go *slowwwww* up the slide."

"Thanks for the tip, Bart," says Jan. "Got any others while your mouth is still warm?"

"Not right this minute. Fixing Mohammed's boat at the moment, which takes years of practice, astonishing expertise, phenomenal skill, undeniable talent…"

"And bloody good looks?" says Jan. Bart peers over the glasses at the end of his nose, looking pleased. "That too," he says.

I rub the waterline that has formed on the hull of our boat. It changes from a solid paste into bright green specks on the sponge. I hold it out to Jan and say, "Is this algae?"

"Algae and nastiness," says Bart, interrupting, "and it's caused by high levels of phosphates in the water." It's the third time he's had to repair the fitting but he is calm today. Jan has not seen him in a fit, cursing roundly as he flings his hat on the floor and stomps on it.

Today, he tells us that the run-off from every idiot washing their car in the street on a Sunday morning flows down the storm-water drain and into the river. Jan hasn't heard this before, but I have. He repeats it regularly. "All the crap drifting down from the informal settlements." His voice is rising in intensity. I wish I did not feel embarrassed by old Bart.

He plucks at the pad of foam he is glueing down to prevent the formation of pressure sores. "The phosphates are what make the plants grow cyanobacteria – that's the photosynthetic micro-organisms containing chlorophyll. You could say the bacterium and algae clump together in a symbiotic relationship."

Although Jan knows this better than most, she nods respectfully. She replaces her blades on the rack with the spoons facing the same way as all the others. Mohammed waits while Bart tinkers with a spanner.

"Two or three years back those phosphates were coming from the sewage works leaking into the vlei, but the council sorted that out. About fucking time, too. But the pelicans and flamingos are back. They thrive on the cyanobacteria."

Our boat shed is close to the water's edge. Maybe 100 metres. Doesn't the dishwashing liquid we use to clean our boats seep down through the sand and leak back into the vlei? Has Bart considered this? Does Jan? What does Mohammed think of water conservation, if he even thinks about it? He lives in Delft, a windswept township on the Flats. He has to take taxis, travelling for hours, smoking while he waits for somebody to pick him up and fold the wheelchair into the boot of their car for the final trip from Busy Corner to the yacht club.

I read academic papers on microbial diversity and ecology by Canadian academics. *Owing to their hostile nature the soda lakes are often remote from the main centers of human activity and perhaps for this reason they have been little studied.*

"And for the record," says Bart, waving a spanner at us, "those phosphates are highly corrosive. They'll chew up all the metal fittings if you don't wash that boat properly. So, girlies, make sure you do."

Jan rolls her eyes. I pull my cap down and stifle a giggle. If you don't concentrate while wiping the shell, you rip open your knuckles on the bolts.

Jan goes over my training programme with me for the week ahead. She throws her towel over a trestle and demonstrates how I'm to replicate the technique in the boat on the ergo at the gym. "For a sharp catch," she says, her chin tucked in, neck long. "Engage your lats and lift your sternum. Watch your posture. Sit up straight."

Mohammed watches Jan. Her email is not on the club list yet, but it will be if she joins as a member. Jan is saying I must improve my cardiovascular fitness, telling me how to balance this with strength training. That means I must lose weight, which she doesn't say directly. She advises me to research the Paleo Diet, to look at the CrossFit videos. "Check it out online," she says. "There's tons of information. Look up 'Mark's daily apple', while you're at it. He has interesting ideas on nutrition."

I want to say, Google is your friend, but it sounds lame.

Lame? I catch Mohammed's eye and wince. He winks at me, as if he's read my mind and forgiven me for having an able body while being soft in the head. Mohammed wheels himself to the public library, about four kilometres from his house. Last time he was here, he had pressure sores that smelled foul. Today they have healed up, so he can get out on the water again.

Bart, having finished the repair to Mohammed's boat, pushes it on a dolly down to the water.

"Kom, tjommie," says Jan. With her Scottish accent, it sounds funny. Mohammed and I laugh at her. She pushes the wheelchair over the rough ground, without ramming it, without it getting stuck. He adjusts his cap. I carry his blades, his water bottle and towel.

Bart hoists Mohammed into the boat after aligning the punts. Jan and I wave him off and wish him a nice row. When she says goodbye to me, she pats my shoulder, says, "You're making great progress." She drives off in an old blue Conquest and I stroke my shoulder where she touched me. Today, when I look up the nutritional advice Jan recommended, I will find some rowing jokes for Mohammed. I will send him a link.

You Pay for the View:
Twenty Tips for Super Pics

1. Hold it Steady

December 1975 – Hermanus

BENEATH THE CHRISTMAS TREE that tilted in the empty fireplace lay four identically sized presents, one for each of us. The gift tag with my name on it read: *Wishing you many happy memories, love Mum*. It was almost the size of a *Princess Tina Ballet Book*. On discovering a ring-backed self-adhesive photograph album, my heart sank. At least we were all getting the same dull thing.

The smallish box-shaped gift was a mystery: *Hope this gives years of fun, Dad*. It could be anything. My father wanted me to guess. Whatever it was, it wasn't the satin pointe shoes I'd begged for. I crossed my fingers for a jewellery box with a wind-up ballerina twirling an endless pirouette into angled mirrors. It seemed unlikely. The thing was solid, heavy.

My father's eyes shone as I pulled a Kodak Brownie Reflex camera with a meniscus lens and rotary shutter from the wrapping paper. It fit into a brown leather holder that closed with a press stud. At eight, I struggled to look pleased as he opened the latch and pulled the film holder out in order to slot the roll of film into the camera, but he didn't notice. He explained why a film should only ever be loaded in subdued light, inside, and never in the dazzling sunshine. He let me turn the winding knob, advancing the film, until a small hand with a pointing finger appeared in the red window at the back.

Ride the Tortoise

My interest grew when I lifted the flip-up cover and stared into the viewfinder, a two-inch square of glass. I watched my sisters reduced in size, catching balls and carrying their dolls. In miniature they sounded quieter, somehow.

The baby, crawling out the door, let her head hang down to the step below. I thought it would be a good shot, it had made us laugh at the time, but the developed prints were disappointing. The baby's head was a blurry rock. In all the images the light was harsh and the figures washed out. The photos of the budgie and the beach were indistinguishable from one another. In black and white, you couldn't tell that the blotches on my sister's dress were polka dots the same red as the cocktail tomatoes growing in our garden, fruits that sprayed pips down one's front. My two middle sisters stared at me as if being scolded. One glared over a fan that Father Christmas brought her, a fan I would have danced with, had I received it.

Years later, on unpacking a bookshelf to paint the wall behind it, I rediscover the old album, its paisley sateen cover grubby from handling. The plastic sheet no longer sticks. A photo of my sister slips out.

She wears a pale leotard and matching tulle skirt falling over her out-turned knee, holding a pose on the lawn with her foot aligned. Long delicate fingers lift above her head. The other hand rests, balanced on her shoulder.

2. Move in Closer
28 April 1992 – Constantiaberg Clinic, Cape Town

My first sighting of my daughter some hours after her birth was in the prints. Delivered at 28 weeks, she was twelve weeks premature. With my right hand rendered useless by the antibiotic drip, and my left too floppy to hold photographs, much less my child in the neonatal ICU, my husband held the

41

images, angling them for me to see. He held them proudly, careful about fingerprints on the glossy finish.

I wanted to pound against his chest, but my head was a melon on the pillow, the searing in my belly, sharp stones. I remembered squatting on the grass for the first time without a nappy, compelled to examine what my body had produced. Now I stared at the pictures, horrified, avidly inspecting this thing I had excreted.

My daughter's face was invisible behind a mask of tubes and pipes. Her blood-specked body was attached to wires, and her chest dipped under a fluted rib cage. Her father told me what the doctor had told him, that she'd been a breech delivery, still high in my womb. He'd had to wrestle her downwards, hence her deeply bruised limbs.

Her swollen sex captured on film was pornographic. It angered me, but I couldn't stop looking. I resented this theft of intimacy and my inadequate womb equally. The envelope of prints grew ratty from being clutched. I handled each picture of the child I couldn't hold, fearful that each view might be the last.

Five days later, a tall Dutch nurse wheeled me to the incubator. She took my hands in hers, turning them over, positioning them side-by-side to form a tiny cradle in my lap. She covered my hands in a soft cloth, then deftly placed my daughter, still attached to the cables, into my palms.

The bones of her skull shifted beneath her skin like tectonic plates made of eggshell. Her torso filled my other hand. Her eyes rolled in opposite directions, never meeting mine.

3. Kill the Flash
January 1998 – Bryanston, Sandton, Alexandra
Behind the lens I was possessed. I stood between the cars on Jan Smuts Avenue at sunset for a feature on traffic for

the weekly community paper, where I'd landed my first job. I composed drivers' faces that squinted in the low light, homeward bound. To catch the taillights, red as the sky, I turned my back to the drivers for their silhouette, impervious to danger.

When the circus came to town, the elephant enclosure caught my eye. I unclipped the flash and edged in slowly to avoid startling the beast. The deep creases in its skin, the bright circle of its eye drew me in. A group of children gathered at the gate, keen for adventure. The elephant looked primal. It flapped its ears, but I had superpowers. The right shot would make front page. I worked the angle, pulling in closer. Disengaging eventually from the viewfinder to put in a new roll of film, I snapped from my trance. The children had followed me in. We were all too close.

I backed away slowly, imagining a trampling. It would be my first blood on the job. The only reporter on the scene, I might even crack the dailies. The keeper ushered the intruders out with firm instructions. The elephant eyed me through its lashes, ancient as an archetype, turned to its trough and farted.

When the editor wanted a photo of the changing face of the city, I slipped into a building site after hours, ignoring the warning signs. I hopped over mounds of bricks, scampering across setting concrete and up unfinished stairs. I climbed onto the scaffolding for the best vista, pulling myself up to the unstable planks on the uppermost ledge. My editor would be ecstatic. I'd be a legend.

The scaffolding swayed. I clung to the ledge, trying to slide back to safety, but too afraid to step back. When I called my husband on the cell phone, he said I was a silly goose. Go back the same way you went up. Going up had been easy. I'd been watching the sky.

Bodyguards accompanied us when we entered the township of Alexandra with the executive team from the Chamber of Commerce. Leaning out the open window of the jeep, I photographed the ghetto, its power lines and glistening sewers. Unperturbed by the passing warlords waving guns to assert their domain, I protected my camera but not my ear as I landed on the floor of the vehicle. "Eish, Miss Smarty Pants," said the exasperated city councillor, who had yanked me back inside. "You'll be the big shot in your coffin?"

She was right. It wasn't the camera that had made me brave. It was the pills that had dulled my wits and made me foolish. Ambition made me reckless. But there had been no girls in the Bang Bang Club, and the political violence was over anyway.

4. Mix Up Your Perspective
June 1999 – Craighall Park, Johannesburg
He gave me assignments: look for the texture of the tuna, the reflection off a boot. He spoke of shutter speeds and apertures, focal length and depth of field, but no words stayed, no instructions stuck. They were as disconnected as the sunbeams floating in my window that I'd tried to capture. He was a good teacher, but my thoughts fired, hot and bright, exploding sparklers turning to smoky ash.

I called through the darkroom curtain, telling him I was afraid. He said, "You have to engage through the lens, embrace your subject. You can't stand outside." I stared at the floor, noting the shimmering grease stains, wanting to know how to capture them forever. He unpegged my black-and-white images from the line where they had dried in curved oblongs. There were no delicate points of incandescence, no subtle interplay of light and shadow, only dullness, smudgy and out of focus.

He was a Buddhist and tolerant of my failings. When the company accountants decided it was time to go digital, he said it was karma. At first film was rationed. Then the darkroom was closed. No more experiments. Before driving off in his battered El Camino, he gave me a present: two images overlaid on the same print with an embossed pattern forming the border. He explained the process. He explained again. He smelled of pickling chemicals. His words wouldn't stick. I forgot as fast as I heard. It was the pills. I couldn't even remember his name, but he taught me to see.

5. Take Posed Shots into Candid Territory
February 1998 – Sandston, Johannesburg

The camera is a licence to sit on the floor, dress badly, stand on tables, climb on chairs. It intrudes, jockeying up to VIPs, disturbing, devotional. It is a ticket to the front row, a licence to jump protocol. It is permission to stare at folk who are dreaming of kissing. A go-ahead to notice them picking their scabs. Watch them weeping. A valid disguise, it drives and devours. It closes in, desiring to subject the subject to unspeakable vulnerability. It begs for objection. It invokes silliness, pulled faces, rude signs, tipped glasses. It invites the subject to kick up a fuss, shuck their shoes, dive wild. Kneel in public. Tip into submission. Succumb to the tilted.

6. Include People
25 November 2006 – Dullstroom, Mpumalanga

We are driving to Hoedspruit, Linda, Mvuyo and I, a six-hour journey to a week-long writing workshop. A custody battle with my ex is raging, and I think I'm dying. We arrive at a truck stop for petrol and coffee. Sharp orange cannas burst into the wide blue sky alongside an abandoned reservoir, where long grass cracks the brittle concrete. The ridiculous joy of the flowers commands my lens. I want the image, but it's more than wanting. I want a record of this trip to pin to my notice board when we get back, reminders that this day happened. I want proof that I journeyed through these places despite my bleak mood.

Mvuyo removes his jacket. On the front of his T-shirt: *You cannot teach a man a lesson...* On the back: *by shooting him in the head.* When I focus on stairs, the kerb, or a fuel truck, the camera doesn't intrude. It's not even a rudeness, but when I focus on people, my own need shames me. Mvuyo's shirt is priceless. How else to remember it when my memory is a doddery tramp, blinking against the sun?

At first I kill the flash and snatch the shot from behind Mvuyo. Later I snap from the side, pretending to focus on the poppies blooming outside the thatched cottage where he stands. It's disingenuous, but I'm still summoning up the courage to do it full frontal. I can't decide whether I feel like an exhibitionist, holding a phallus, or a voyeur observing something never intended for my eyes.

Later, sipping tea in a coffee shop, I notice the small print on his T-shirt: *Wake up with a proverb.* I ask if he minds that I took his photo. He tells me that in Swaziland, where he comes from, the old men believe that each photograph hastens your death by a day. His voice is level, but I can't tell whether his expression is amused or pissed. "Every shot," he says, "steals another breath."

I've just stolen two weeks of his life. I promise to delete the entire file. If I erase the images, will he get his fortnight back?

7. *Put the Sun Behind You*
2 January 2007 – Cape Point, Western Cape
We climb to the Cape Point lighthouse in the December

46

heat, a brick of dread in my belly with each laboured step. I want just one decent memento of this so-far uncomplicated day. If I ask them to pose, my children will grin with thin lips, tight jaws. If I promise extra pocket money, they might cooperate. I beg them to be natural.

The colours are perfect: her coal-black jeans and silver-speckled top, his orange T-shirt, the gradated blues of the sky and sea. I take, take, take until my memory card is full. There's always a spoiler: sunshine kissing only one child's face, the other squinting away, a tourist's butt protruding into an otherwise faultless shot. My daughter will not eat. Before she gets any thinner, I want an enlargement, to remember her like this.

8. *Consider Variety*
21 March 2007 – Blairgowrie, Johannesburg
The list of things I want to remember when we move to Canada grows as I plan what to ship and what to leave. There's the trinket box from my late mother-in-law, books that I'll never reread but hate to part with, baby clothes I hand-embroidered, and the children's first drawings – when we still approximated a happy family.

I could keep some as electronic memories, pixels on my computer. Others will remain as electrical impulses coursing ever more faintly along my neural pathways. The list grows at night. In the dark I touch the different textures on the bed: the rough wool blanket, the satin trim on the pillowslip beneath my fingernails, the once puffy duvet, too light on my shoulders. Can my skin imprint this tactile dance for its own memory, or does it need visual clues?

The faux baroque frame of an oil painting glints silver in the streetlight. The subject, which by daylight is a Renaissance woman leaning into a pink rose, is a black expanse of unlit canvas in the dark. Only her pale hands and upturned nose reflect. I try not to like this painting so much. We won't have space in a tiny apartment.

In the morning light, the contours of covers thrown back and wrinkled sheets are a study. By mid-afternoon, when the bed is neatly made and its plump cushions have been set straight, shadowed stripes will fall through the slatted wooden footboard onto the folded navy blanket.

Will we take the blue-and-white floral curtains that once hung in my mother's dining room? No. Those I must photograph. Perhaps lying beneath them, catching the knife pleats and a reflection in the window. But the view beyond – how will I frame the hoopoes and hadedas that feast on the lawn, the red clivia berries fattening on green stalks beneath the acacia?

The burgundy Persian rug trails black woollen snakes from its fraying edge. So pretty on the reddish teak of the parquet tiles, it almost glows when the long light of the summer solstice floods the house. Will the floors ever feel as solid in Canada? Can a photo of our Johannesburg floor ever be sturdy enough in a new country?

9. *Take Your Camera Everywhere*
28 March 2007 – Melville, Johannesburg

With my bag in the boot of the car, it was impossible to capture the roadside vendor on the pavement kneeling over his wares. Against the backdrop of a brilliant green hedge, he pondered the placement of a final orange atop his pyramid of fruit.

"Support, Mami, support," he sang, flashing teeth as white as a cliché. He boogied over to my window, proffering an orange, trusting I'd buy. Nigerian, I guessed, with that blue-black skin. Or Congolese? The locals would no doubt slander him, calling him a tsotsi, a criminal. They would call him makwerekwere – he who speaks with a clacking tongue.

A year later I will pass this intersection during the height of the xenophobic pogroms erupting in the country, and I will wonder if the orange-seller escaped the scourge. I will wonder about the photographers capturing images of the hideous fire dance, while disaffected locals scream, "Buyelekhaya!" Go back home.

10. Shoot Lots
March 2007 – Forbes Road, Blairgowrie

There are many pictures I mean to take. Mina's skin, the colour of cocoa, gleaming as she walked round the park. "Kea slim-a. I am slimming," she would say.

She used to work two houses down at number eight, where Jet, the collie, barked when we passed. After work she'd sit on the other side of the road with Gogo, the matriarch of the domestic workers in the area. Mina and Gogo inhaled snuff from the same small tin, laughing and dabbing their eyes with the brown stained tissues balled in their pockets.

In her spare time, Mina made rainbow quilts with matching cushion covers. She also mended hems and broken zips. She sang in a rich alto in Sotho, translating for me: Jesus's love never failed me yet.

I wish I'd got a photo of her spinning the ancient Singer, black as a prayer book with silver fittings. I never got a photo of the bright geometry of her handiwork and the light on her Vaselined lips when she smiled. But it was her good luck to move on: thieves leaped the fence last week, holding guns to the new owner's head, stealing his car.

Gogo told me about the attack as I walked home, carrying the kindling I'd gathered in the park for the evening fire. I walked on up the street, where I met Vinnie and Molise, our other new neighbours, outside their home. I told them the bad news, urging them to be careful when they returned in the dark. "It's true," they said. "Our uncle was burgled last week in Kelvin. We are waiting for a lift to the wake. We are going to pray." I wished I still had the language for that.

11. Know Your Range
23 April 2007 – Oliver Tambo International Airport, Johannesburg

They shimmy away from me and swing from the loopholds as the shuttle bus lurches out of the terminus. I walk behind them on the runway, unzipping my camera case. A photo could be beautiful: the dawn sky is a dove grey, tinted orange, the nose of the aeroplane behind them, my daughter carrying her guitar. Because the flash setting is still on, the focus in the dimness is slow. By the time the shutter opens, they're pulling silly faces. Useless. Going up the stairs, they jostle each other, laughing.

I sit between them in the plane, an old habit from when they were small, but now they're both taller than I am. My son passes his cell phone to his sister over my head. She titters, sending it back. I ask what they're looking at.

"Just a snowman," says my daughter.

Probably Kama Sutra, winter-style. "Is that snowman up to smut?"

"No!" she squeals, meaning yes. What to do, what to do? I should confiscate the phone. My son sniggers. His breath smells like gherkins.

"Did you brush your teeth?" I know the answer. "Did you bring your toothbrush?" I know the answer. "Did you eat breakfast?" No answer.

I've petered out before lift-off. When I refuse to buy my son a chocolate muffin from the food cart, saying, "Breakfast was your responsibility," he buys his own. His mood switches. His angry profile is so like his father's that I wince. As we come in to land, I lean in past him to point my lens at the back of Table Mountain. He pulls away from my touch.

"I'm sorry," I say, unsure why I'm apologising.

12. *Be a Picture Director*
27 April 2007 – Wynberg, Cape Town

We vacation at the home of my parents, the hoarders, where every room is afflicted by clutter: each ledge and shelf has too many things; tables and desks balance piles of paper and towers of books; drawers are crammed with stuff. Each nook contains too much clobber.

Earrings drop off edges, coins roll under beds, paper clips collect in knick-knack holders and pens in cracked coffee cups. Boxes and clocks fill the tops of cupboards; tools congregate in corners. Even the garage is a shambles.

Every night I wake sweating from a dream that my children are climbing a mountain of empty bottles. They get smaller and smaller until they fall between the cracks and are swallowed in the recycling, where brown and green and clear glass are tossed and boiled together. Only their voices are big, like giants' teeth chattering and echoing in the dark skip, but I can't understand their words.

With my parents away I take pictures of their house, because the camera never lies. Even though it's a disloyalty, it's a warning to myself, a private reminder that I sip the same soup. I want to spit out this heritage because even as I sneak around snapping their mess, my own unopened mail languishes on shelves with unread magazines and unreturned library books. It might already be too late to terminate this tendency. While my surfaces might be clear, the closets back home are another story, burgeoning with the unworn, the unwanted, the unloved.

Liesl Jobson

13. Lock the Focus
27 April 2007 – Blairgowrie, Johannesburg

He wolfs down the cereal, toast, eggs, but an hour later, in a gravelly bass: "Ma, what's for lunch?" My gangly son, the youngest in his class; the tallest too. At twelve years, he wears size eleven soccer boots, a moustache on the way, taking pills for the spots that appeared this year beside his freckles. He'll be six foot and then some. The paws of the cub show the height of the lion. Sometimes he's so beautiful. Other times too much like his father, especially the lips that disapprove without a word. Those are the images I scrap. Then the phone call. An "incident" at school. He's bliksemed a kid – a bigger one, at least. Both are sent home with bloody noses. At the weekend I stroke the cheek below his swollen eye. It is a question, but he won't talk. I don't push. The school has dealt with this already. His father too. I say, "You have to mind the line." He nods, tears in his eyes.

14. Get Down on Their Level
30 April 2007 – Parkview, Johannesburg

At Moyo the waiters wear ostrich-feather crowns and curlicues of white dots painted on their black faces. My camera pulses in my pocket, but my son is rocking his chair in the gravel, bumping the table. His sister says, "Quit being a doofus." I say, "Guys, please, manners." She slides the menu out of his reach.

The Wishy-Washy lady arrives with scented rosewater, warmed for the ritual washing. She dips into a half-kneel, singing as she pours the warm water over our hands: "Izandla ziyagezana." One hand washes the other. It's a proverb, similar to I scratch your back, you scratch mine. My mother's voice is dinging in my head: *translate the song for the children; distract them from their spat; this is a golden opportunity to teach them about their heritage, multiculturalism; wake up.*

But I do not. They are hungry and scowling, not open to lectures on heritage or language or Zulu proverbs. Before we left home, I'd told them we'd only be ordering drinks; the restaurant is pricey. I offered each a sandwich so they wouldn't be hungry. They'd refused, saying it was too early to eat.

I remind them I am out of work. My daughter says, "You pay for the view." The cappuccinos arrive sprinkled with cinnamon; the milkshakes have a swirl of cream topped with a coffee bean. More loudly she says, "This place is a tourist trap." Instead of simply pulling my shawl tighter, I chide her when the waiter leaves: "That may be so, but at least the restaurant is creating employment, helping folk earn a living. You don't have to put it down."

Tears ripen in her eyes. She snatches her sunglasses. She didn't intend all that. She was trying out new words, like she did at three and four, when I'd clap my hands with delight. At fifteen, she still wants me to notice things like the new ear piercing, or the cherry-red bra strap peeking out her black top. She hopes I'll laugh, or raise an impressed eyebrow. I stretch across the table to pat her hand, wanting to comfort and apologise, but my gesture is too clumsy. She pulls away, still injured. I take out my camera and point it at a tree growing skew.

15. *Move it From the Middle*
30 April 2007 – Parkview, Johannesburg
The vacant bench at Zoo Lake tolerates my insecurity and dithering; it waits while I shift my settings, change focus, try angles and apertures. It has no memory of other photographers making it look bad, doesn't harp on about being unphotogenic, doesn't assume unnatural poses, or

blink at the flash. It doesn't expect me to know what I'm doing, never even asks what kind of camera I have. While I figure what belongs in the composition, the bench is eternally patient, unashamed of its emptiness. I shouldn't be ashamed of my own, approaching from behind, pretending I'm not here.

16. Search for Details
2 May 2007 – Sandton

The pelts of a cow, a kudu, a springbok and a zebra hang on a line between two trees at the turn-off to Tara, the state mental hospital. The spot is on the main route to Hartbeespoort Dam, and tourists stop to haggle.

Six years ago I was admitted from a private hospital because my medical insurance was exhausted. It was a month after the attack and I couldn't talk or sleep. I alternated between trying to throw furniture out the window in the middle of the night and wanting to lie down on the highway. I need to go through the hospital gates again, to be outside looking in. Maybe if I had pictures of the low bungalow with the padded cell, I could figure out how I got there in the first place.

The memories are slivers: a young German intern with striped socks and brown corduroys studying my transfer documents, muttering in a heavy accent, This is not right, this is not right, you have to see the Professor; the lone Ethiopian guinea fowl that limped amidst the flock of local birds, which the Professor pointed out; the light falling through the thinning oak trees in patterns like crocheted lace; the queue for medication; the tremor in my jaw; the wailing, the wailing.

The sun shone in wide bands through the long windows of the women's ward when the shutters were open, and in narrow stripes when they closed. It was a balmy autumn and my lover bought me a canary, orange as a mango. The pet-shop owner promised the bird would sing like Pavarotti. He hung the cage from a bent coathanger hooked to the rafters of the ward's deep veranda. When the ward director said the bird had to go, hospital regulations, I thought he was joking.

I want to go back there to see how far I've really come in six years, but my curiosity makes me squeamish. I drive past the gate and return to the cow, the kudu, the springbok and the zebra, snapping them like a tourist instead. When the vendor urges me to buy one, I lie, saying I'm vegetarian.

17. Position the Horizon
4 May 2007 – St Stithians, Randburg

The images playing over and over are more vivid than if they were enlarged to fit the sky. They rouse me, sweating and lurching in the middle of the night, repeating on the viewscreen of my mind: that morning I raced to the school, the look on the cleaning woman's face – was it horror, pity, or judgement? With her bucket and mop, she cleaned up the blood that had sprayed over the girls' bathroom.

Then the oozing crosshatches slashed on my daughter's thighs and calves, her eyes bleary. I wondered if she was stoned, if she was dying. Her voice saying, "Why are *you* here? Why *you*?"

The bug-eyed guidance teacher wearing lilac eyeshadow returns each night, leaning in too close, saying, "This is a cry for help. Don't you *know*? You really should *do* something this time. Get your girl some help."

And the nurse in the emergency room saying, "My name is Romy," as she removes wads of toilet paper from the wounds. As she peels it off, the parallel gashes trickle, trickle. My daughter asks if it will hurt. I count the cuts, losing track at sixteen on one arm alone, estimate a hundred covering her body. The nurse reassures her; it's only water. When she notices the tears in my eyes, she tells me it's time to go wait outside.

There's the doctor's rage – the woman who stitched and stitched her. "She narrowly missed an artery." The beautiful doctor with skin like white linen and eyes like blue glass.

Two weeks later, stepping out the shower, I see my daughter naked for the first time, waiting her turn to wash. On each leg is a band of livid purple scars like barbed-wire wreaths around her upper thighs.

These are the images that don't go away. I'm told that, like the scars, they will fade with time, but in the silence before the first birdsong, it is too soon to say.

18. *Look Your Subject in the Eye*
June 2007 – Bryanston, Inanda, Houghton

When my son is promoted to the second team, I attend the match, just a week after my daughter's discharge from hospital. It's held at Bryandale, but I get muddled and go to Bryaneven. When I finally arrive, I'm so jumpy that I drop a teacup, which breaks on the concrete. I keep my camera in my bag, afraid I'll drop it too. The match is a good one. My boy defends three goals. They win.

The next match is on a cool Saturday morning at St David's. I get a few shots of him jostling with his team on the stands beforehand, but my battery dies as they take the field. He runs forward to the ball, kicking with a powerful swing, his toe level with his shoulder, opposite hand flung forward. His teammates cheer. They win 3–0.

Next is a home game against Redhill. I arrive at 3pm for the 3.30 match, but when I find my son, he has played early. I buy him a Coke and leave, wishing I could take him with me.

The following one is on a bright afternoon, just after his father and I are called to the school. His teachers are concerned about his behaviour, his poor attitude. Other kids find his completed assignments and hand them in for him. He looks sad in class. Only the soccer coach says he is doing well.

In the pictures from that match, my son slouches against the goal posts, scowling with embarrassment at his mother with her camera. His team boxes the ball in on the far side of the field, scoring goal after goal. There's little chance of getting him in action. I photograph two boys from the first team practising fancy footwork on the sideline, moving like dancers.

When the ball finally crosses the mid-line and he gets a great header, my camera strap is in the way. When his long limbs execute an elegant drop kick, I'm in the wrong spot. At half-time he tells me the first team goalie is injured. "Maybe I'll get to play with the firsts," says my boy, eyes bright. He leaps about, imagining mock lunges.

In the second half, I get one distant shot of him catching the ball. The image isn't sharp and then the match is over, a hollow victory over a weak team. Trudging along the white lines heading for the change room, the coach pats him on the back, saying, "You'll be a great goalie soon," but he chooses another boy to defend the firsts.

The next match I attend they are challenging KES, their fiercest competition to date. The game keeps my son on his toes, but I've forgotten my camera. He defends well, diving at their feet throughout the game. As the final goal bounces out from his arms and into the net, his team loses. He strikes his head in frustration, again and again. In the car going home, he sits eyes closed. I say something about doing better next time.

"There won't be a next time, Mom," he says. The motor

revs too high on the steep downhill of Munro Drive. I brake as the car twists around the cliff face, wanting to look at him. What is he saying? The car behind is too close. My heart races. My voice isn't level: "What do you mean?"

"That was the last match of the season. It's athletics after half-term." He hates athletics.

"There's always next year. What about high school?"

"We play rugby in high school."

"There's no soccer team?"

"There is, but soccer's not cool."

"Rugby is problematic." I think broken bones. Concussion. Paralysis.

"Ma," he says, "get a life."

I watched every match of the 1994 World Cup soccer tournament from my bed, while he kicked inside me, threatening premature labour. The amniocentesis promised a boy, a normal boy. I craved spanspek melons and spinach. I nibbled on figs and ginger, praying he'd stay inside me a little longer. A week, please. Another day. Everything after 28 weeks was a bonus.

19. Use a Plain Background

15 June 2007 – Constitution Hill, Braamfontein

I go to the coffee shop at the Old Fort – the jail where Gandhi and later Mandela were held – on the way home from the doctor. It's been six weeks since my daughter hurt herself and now my son seems to be slipping. I wake from nightmares of war zones: soldiers, overturned personnel carriers, dismembered bodies. The diagnosis is post-traumatic stress, the prescription anti-depressants.

This is where apartheid's most sadistic prison officers imposed their warped minds on blacks brought in for petty offences like failing to carry their passbooks. They were made to line up naked,

jump in the air several times, and, on landing, bend over to have
their rectums inspected for smuggled items.

The old cells have been transformed into a conference
venue where historical photographs are enlarged on glass;
the original stable is a reception room, but ghosts of cane
and rubber still hover, even on the sunniest day.

A flogging frame towers over visitors in the tiny
exercise courtyard, and a plaque explains how prisoners
were strapped to it before receiving their punishment.
Just visible above the high stone walls are the uppermost
flats of Hillbrow's nearby apartment blocks. The parents
of political detainees rented these flats so that they could
watch their children through binoculars when they were
let out to exercise.

Inside the cells, the light stabs onto the red concrete
floor from high barred windows, bouncing off the chipped
white tiles around the lavatory. Shadows of the heavy
doors fall on the peeling paint and cracked steps.

I don't know enough about working in low light;
haven't yet figured out how my digital camera works.
The instructions translated from Japanese are strange,
with menus "expressing option of disconnect". The
manufacturer's website yields more information than I can
process. I will find somebody to talk me through the jargon
when I can concentrate again, when my logic recovers.

I point and shoot at the guardhouse, the lattices of
barbed wire, skyscrapers above the ramparts, and a spiny
succulent growing on the sheer face of the rock.

20. *Watch the Light*
June 2007 – Blairgowrie, Johannesburg
In the bleak days after my daughter's cutting, my
godfather and his wife, keen amateur photographers, pass
briefly through Joburg. After twenty years in Wisconsin,

his accent is still a clear Grahamstown, hers a lilting Roedean. I wish my visitors could hear my daughter sing and watch my son offering unprompted to help at the table, but their father has custody, and their routine cannot be disrupted. Not even for overseas visitors. So I open to the pictures of my girl strumming her guitar, head back and happy, another of her leaning against a lamppost at the Waterfront, pretty in the wind; then show them my boy on an ornamental lion, another of him braced at the goal post, waiting for the ball.

It's the first truly cold night of the year, and we add logs to the fire while the food warms. We wait for my new husband to get back from work and I try to ignore how my ribs feel stapled to my spleen. I pour my guests wine, but don't drink lest I drown.

I say, "I can't get the long view on this." It's like I've survived a car accident without a single inky bruise to show. I'm a mourner with no gravestone to visit.

But their presence is a balm, and I show the pictures I took at the women's jail, the old fort, the roadside memorial that always has fresh flowers. Over dinner we chat about the language of photography, the aggressive hunting terminology: take, capture and catch. Terms of weaponry: shoot, strike and sightlines. These hard-hitting male sports and their warrior words annoy. My godfather says, "Try saying 'make' an image instead." It's a feminine word, empowering, a verb of creation. "Might help you feel less like you've taken something that's not yours." He suggests seeing myself as a graphic artist, drawing with light. "Play a little," says his wife. "Think of the camera as a toy."

After they leave, I wait for the fire to burn down before going to bed. I reach for my camera, remembering another fire, the blacksmith at a forge, how he twirled birds and butterflies out of molten iron. I remember the hoof-print tattoo down the back of his legs, his leather sandals moving in and out of focus in the dust, and the growing excitement as I sensed that a great shot was on track. I remembered the thrill of opening the images and finding the pic was everything I wanted. And more. There were lines I hadn't anticipated, movement I never planned.

I remove the cap. Polish the lens with my skirt and lie close enough to be comfortable. Zoom in, zoom out. I frame the flames, tinkering with the adjustments. I think about the lenses I trust, the comfort of settling in behind the camera. If heat bends light, does that explain this sense of knowing what I'm doing?

I slow the shutter; open the rest.

The last log on the fire flares over the grate. When I open the images in the morning, the familiar delight is back. The sparks, invisible to me in the viewfinder the night before, fly upward in skittering trails. Shooting stars from the hearth dance out into the dark.

On a
Broomstick

RINA STARES AT THE LIVER SPOTS on the back of her hands. The darkened patches are the same chocolaty colour as the thread she is using to adjust her husband's cummerbund. The brown is not ideal against the black fabric, but she doesn't have time to buy more black thread, and she reasons that the stitches will be concealed. It's not as if he'll be dancing.

Boeta, her six-year-old, cocks his head, then snips the length of thread with the scissors in a precise and delicate action.

"Thanks, son," she says.

"When can I help you again?" he asks as he hops from one foot to the other, waving the scissors about.

"As soon as I've finished this stitching, you can snip the thread again," she says. She enfolds his hand containing the scissors and pries them away gently. The last time Jacques wore his dinner jacket was at his retirement function, which coincided with the twins' twenty-first birthday. He had decided to celebrate the double event in style. "Not too shabby," he'd said as they drove down the tree-lined entrance to the Mount Nelson Hotel where the festivities took place. The event brought relatives together from around the country – and it took nine months to settle the credit card bill.

Jacques had looked like a wildebeest that night. His great mop of hair, which shook when he laughed, had been silver-grey, streaked with brown, and his skin was radiant and tanned. He'd twirled her round the dance floor, his hand firm in the small of her back and said, "If I was twenty-one, I'd marry you all over again." She was glad he didn't ask, "Would you?"

How long ago was that? A year? Eighteen months? She couldn't remember, but now his dinner jacket is three sizes too big and his head is bald. He shaved off his hair before it fell out, saying he was perfecting the art of cool, like Koos and Danie.

"Gotta go the whole way, Pops. Get the body piercing too," said Koos. She knew it was an attempt at humour, to smooth over the gruesome truth, but she hadn't even pretended to laugh.

The twins' body piercing had been a sore point. The boys had dared each other over too many beers at the Junkyard one February afternoon when the waves at Muizenberg were too calm to surf and the sand shimmered in the heat. While they should have been sitting in a first-year Engineering lecture, they were picking out barbells and being instructed on how to keep their wounds clean. When they returned home that evening, Danie's tongue was too swollen to eat and he lisped when he spoke. Koos kept prodding the silver stud perched above his eyebrow.

"You didn't go to some back-yard operation, did you?" asked their mother.

"Hell, no! We did it ourselves," said Koos.

Rina clucked her tongue; Jacques laughed.

"Ag, Ma, we went to Kippie's Paleis," said Koos, patting her on the shoulder. She shrugged off his hand. "It's legit. They used sterile needles and stuff. I watched them open new packets in front of us. We won't get Aids or anything."

"Guess you don't want to see where else we got body art…" said Koos, reaching for his belt buckle. Danie backhanded his brother and said, "Don't talk shit, Koos-face." The boys lurched, raucous with laughter and Amstel, but Rina had paled.

"That's neither clever nor funny," she said, flushing with anger. She did not want to think about what her sons might do with or to their members.

Jacques had stroked her hand across the table, saying, "Poppie, don't sweat the small stuff. Life's pretty short."

Rita had pulled her hand away. "You don't have to encourage their irresponsibility."

Not long afterwards, Jacques began to limp. He'd twist and turn at night, unable to get comfortable, wrestling the duvet, fighting the pillows. She listened to him sighing in the dark, pretending sleep. She wondered, but only briefly, if he was having an affair.

She remembers now how he'd grunted as he took his place at the Sunday dinner table, maneuvering into the heavy chair with difficulty.

"Too much golf?" said Rina, serving roast potatoes.

"Too much retirement," said Jacques, with a note of false jollity. He poured a glass of Meerendal Cabochon, swirling the wine in the glass and inhaling deeply. "I should probably lay off this stuff!"

"You think you may have gout?" Rina asked, setting the last plate down in front of him and taking her place.

"Toppie raak oud," said Koos. *Our father's getting old.*

"Toppie! Toppie!" said Boeta, reaching for a potato with his fingers.

Rina frowned at Koos and said to Boeta, "Wait for grace." They held hands and Jacques gave thanks for health and wealth, family and fellowship.

"Mmmm… Can you smell liquorice and mocha?" said Jacques, holding his wine glass under his nose.

Koos flared his nostrils, sniffed noisily and said in a

professorial tone, "I do believe… a note of… farmyard!"

Boeta giggled.

"Old boots and gooseberries," said Danie. "What can you smell, Ma?"

"Nothing," said Rina, not even reaching for her glass. She'd flavoured the lamb with garlic and rosemary.

"Ag, come on, Poppie," said Jacques. He reached over to pinch her cheek, but winced at the exertion. She sniffed the wine and scowled, saying she couldn't smell a thing. Throughout the meal he shifted in his seat, as if eager to be somewhere else.

After dessert, which Jacques hardly touched, they lay together on their bed. Jacques was in too much pain for their ritual lovemaking. Rina recalled the previous time he'd become edgy and restive. She was eight months pregnant with Boeta when she realised the meaning of his faraway look. She hadn't wanted to acknowledge it, had ignored the clues. She discovered coarse red hairs clinging to the fibres of his suits and jerseys. She wondered about the owner of the long and curly red hair. She wondered which was worse: a no-strings prostitute or a twenty-year-old in the typing pool eager to bag a wealthy husband? She suspected the latter judging by his inattention, the lightness of his step, but didn't have the nerve to ask. Instead, she held up the evidence, saying she damn well hoped he was being careful. Their laatlammetjie didn't need a mother with Aids, didn't need a bastard sibling either.

He'd hung his head in shame, hadn't tried to explain. But a week later, when Rina's blood pressure rocketed and Boeta was delivered three weeks early by emergency Caesarian, Jacques' focus returned. He visited Rina in hospital, bringing flowers and gifts. He cradled the tiny bundled infant against his chest, sleeping in the easy chair beside her. After their discharge, he hovered over Rina, soothing her, preparing meals and measuring out formula into carefully sterilised bottles. He got up for the baby at night and changed nappies. They never discussed his infidelity again. As far as she could tell, it was his sole excursion.

"Doesn't gout usually start in the big toe?"

He wiggled his toes in his socks and sighed, "I'm fine."

"Perhaps you should get Dr Louw to take a look?"

Jacques face twisted, but he said, "Nah, I'll just take a couple of aspirin. I'll be right as rain in a day."

Rina got up to fetch him a glass of water. He tore open the foil strip and swallowed with a gulp. "At least go to the physio," she said. He'd gone for a series of treatments for a few weeks, but it hadn't made much difference. She didn't press him.

Jacques is at the Karl Bremer Hospital. He went in for another treatment yesterday and collapsed. She had watched Koos reverse the car right to the front of the house. Danie held his father's elbow, assisting him down the stairs. They had insisted on taking him, even though Rina had said she would. Jacques told her to stay with Boeta; he said, "Kleinboet needs you." She let them go, figuring they needed time with their father.

"I had a dream, Ma," says Boeta, pressing his Harry Potter figurine onto a miniature Lego broomstick while Rina unpicks the Velcro from Jacques' cummerbund.

"Ja?"

"I dreamed I was playing Quidditch with Pa and Harry Potter. I was behind Pa on our broomstick. We got Harry good."

"That's nice." Rina stares over the top of her glasses, smoothing out the snarl in the thread as it drags through the pleated silk. She has resisted getting bifocals. It is too soon to be old. She will be fifty next month.

Boeta swoops around the kitchen, mimicking the flight path of the dream broomstick. He stops to take a naartjie, but picks up the package of DriNites the hospice visitor had placed on the counter. "What means die-ape-err?" he asks.

"Diaper," she stalls, "is an American word." Rina has avoided discussing Jacques' illness with Boeta.

"Disneyland is in America. What's a diaper?"

"Nappies for grown-ups. Pa needs them because he can't get to the toilet quick-sticks, and it's not nice to have an accident."

"He needs a broomstick to fly there. *Wingardiam leviosa*! That's a spell to make things fly. I know lots of spells."

"That's fine, but don't say them in front of Tannie Marie, okay? It's a secret."

"Ja, Ma," he says in the singsong voice of inattention.

"Please. It's important." Rina's sister runs the Finger of God Coffee Bar and Home Bake. She sells bags of rusks and potholders with "Bless this mess" embroidered in cross-stitch. She plays *Oh the Blood of Jesus* in a continuous loop over the speakers to prevent the lesser demons from invading her shop. She refuses to bake Pokémon or Harry Potter birthday cakes for her clients. Pamphlets about true redemption are freely available on the tables and at the counter.

"Diaper." Boeta traces the letters on the package, sounding out the foreign word.

"You know Pa is terribly sick…"

"Pa's getting better. He's taking us to Disneyland. You and me, and Koos and Danie, after their exams."

Jacques' skin tone had changed. She didn't know precisely what that meant, but it didn't look good. Last month he'd said he was taking Boeta to see a movie. Last month he'd still been able to walk around a shopping centre. When she'd asked what they were going to watch, he'd said they'd see when they got there. Rina thought he'd choose a cartoon, but Boeta insisted on *Harry Potter*. She'd scolded Jacques afterwards, telling him it was inappropriate. She expected the boy to have nightmares, but Boeta was fine.

"Why doesn't Tannie Marie like Harry Potter?" asks Boeta from his vantage point on the floor. Propped up on his elbows on the linoleum, he topples the figurine.

"Maybe he frightens her," says his mother.

"Is my dream a secret too, then?"

"Yes. I think so."

"Is it a good secret or a bad secret?" asks the boy. His mother, distracted, doesn't answer.

"Mevrou says a bad secret is when someone touches your privates, and they tell you it's a secret." Rina nods agreement. "A good secret is a surprise party and you must not tell because it will spoil it. She said if you don't know whether a secret is good or bad, you must ask a grown-up."

"Mevrou has good ideas," says Rina sticking a pin into the pincushion.

The day Dr Louw had held Jacques' X-rays up to the light, pointing out the chondrosarcoma, his face had been a brown study. He had indicated a shady mass at the top of Jacques' femur with his fat black fountain pen, and then he'd slid the images back into the envelope, slow to meet their eyes.

"Amputation is not an option," he said. "We can't remove a hip." As he outlined a daunting treatment plan of radiation and chemotherapy, Jacques had patted Rina's hand, reassuring her.

He'd driven them home and his mood had been breezy. "'n Boer maak 'n plan!" he'd said, *a farmer makes do*. He slapped her buttocks playfully like he'd done when they were newlyweds and he, who had once captained the Boland rugby fifteen, had lifted her effortlessly over the threshold of their new home. He'd insisted on buying the house even though they could ill afford it. He was from farming stock. She'd loved his confidence. A farmer could fix anything.

Rina gently touched his hip. Jacques took her hand, kissing it, and said, "I'll nail this in a month. Just you watch. Then we'll take the guys to America. What do you say?"

Rina said nothing. She calculated the rand-dollar exchange and figured how long it would take to pay off another debt. A week later, she had read about denial in the hospice library.

Boeta replaces the adult nappies on the counter and, taking a naartjie, says, "There's a roller coaster at Disneyland. Danie says a roller coaster is the next best thing to flying." As he sinks his thumb into the centre, the sickly sweet odour of rotten fruit fills the room. Rina looks up, about to say, That doesn't smell right, but he hoots in disgusted fascination and holds it up for her inspection. Pale larvae wriggle in the light.

"Ugh. Disgusting!"

"Meh!" he says, mimicking his brothers.

"Throw it away."

"I'll put it in Pa's new bird-feeder. The loeries will like it." He hops down the back stairs, whistling like his father does to summon the wild birds. Jacques had asked Koos to hang the new feeder near their bedroom window. He liked to watch them swooping in to gather and chatter, competing for the seed. Jacques had taught Boeta the birdcalls of the Piet-my-vrou, the coucal, the barbet, and the hoepoe.

Boeta re-enters the kitchen, wiping the juice off on his dungarees, and says, "Pa said we're going to fly to America. On a plane."

"Sometimes Pa gets things wrong." Rina pins the strip of Velcro on the cummerbund. There was Jacques' self-diagnosis of gout, his refusal to see a doctor until it was too late. There was the financial planner she'd begged him to ditch. She'd never trusted the ex-policeman-turned-investor who had captivated Jacques' imagination. Until his pension vaporised in a scam.

Boeta picks up the DriNites once again. His fingers, tacky from the discarded naartjie, stick to the plastic exterior. He pulls them away slowly, watching the tension of his fingertips distend and relax as the two surfaces peel apart. "We're not really going to go to Disneyland, are we?"

"No," she says, wondering whether he is ready to hear the truth he might already have intuited, unsure of whether she is ready to speak it. "We can't afford to go to Disneyland. Did you wash your hands?"

The boy nods and seats himself beside Rina, says, "I was telling you my dream, Ma, but you weren't listening."

"Tell me again. I'm listening now."

"Pa put me in front of the broomstick and told me to drive. Somehow we changed places in the air so I was in front and Pa behind me, but then he was gone. I could still hear him. I was scared to look around because I didn't want to fall off, but there was Dumbledore, flying away with Pa. They were waving at me. Then I couldn't see Pa. The sun was behind him. I said, wait. I said, come back, the game's not over. Harry Potter called me back to play with him but I couldn't play any more because I'd woken up."

"Eina!" yelps Rina as the needle slips under her fingernail. A large red droplet forms on her fingertip. She presses a tissue under her nail.

"Is Pa coming back from the hospital?" Boeta asks, rearranging the pins in the pincushion. His mother nods, sucking her finger.

"Is he going back to the hospital?"

"Uh-uh. No more treatments."

"Then Pa is getting better. We will go to America."

She pulls a final double stitch and lets Boeta snip the thread for the last time.

"Has Ma got a secret too?" he says, patting the cummerbund.

Rina frowns, plucking a stray thread dangling from his T-shirt, then tousles his hair.

"A secret?" Her limbs feel heavy; her mouth dry.

"Maybe we're having another party at the Mount Nelson?"

"No," she says.

"But you're fixing Pa's belt."

Rina's stomach lurches.

"His cummerbund. Pa says he wants to look snappy when he meets St Peter."

"You said we don't believe in saints."

"Sometimes I get things wrong, too."

Just after they'd received the diagnosis, Rina had told Marie that Jacques would not want to attend the faith healing service at The Finger of God Ministries, but when Marie phoned Jacques directly to ask if he wanted the minister to pray with him, he said, "For sure." Marie and the pastor visited him in hospital, laying their hands on his head, on his feet. Jacques had felt better afterwards, needing less morphine. He asked the pastor to return.

The following day, Jacques asked Rina to take in his tux. Koos had been slouching against the basin in the ward, and Danie was holding his father's hand cautiously, stroking his fingers. A drip administered various medications into a fold of his baggy skin.

"Your tuxedo?" Rina wondered if the drugs were addling his head.

"Face it, Rina, I'm off to the Pearly Gates. And I don't plan to arrive looking shabby."

"What about an eyebrow ring while we're about it," said Koos. "If the pastor can make a hospital visit, why would the body-piercer shy away?"

Danie said, "Pa, you need a tatt, what about, 'Heaven can wait'?"

Jacques swatted Danie weakly. They laughed. Dr Louw couldn't say how long Jacques had. Will he see his sons graduate in three months' time? Will he still be here to hold her hand on her fiftieth birthday?

Rina folds the cummerbund and again takes the scissors away from Boeta, who is stabbing holes in the DriNites. She rubs the pressure mark on the bridge of her nose where her spectacles pinch. Then, gently, she takes Boeta's face between her hands. "Pa's coming back from the hospital tomorrow, but soon he's going to leave us forever."

Boeta pulls away from her grasp. He squats at her feet, lining up Harry beside Dumbledore. "When?" he asks.

"We don't rightly know." She tries to close the lid of the sewing box, but it no longer fits properly. The padded purple silk lining bulges, reminding her of the inside of a coffin.

"Where's he going?"

"To the angels," Rina wipes her face with the back of her sleeve.

"Nah!" says Boeta, shuffling the figures around on the floor.

Rina starts a shopping list: sausages, bread, orange juice, cheese. Boeta rests his head against her knee, and asks, "How will he get there?"

Rina writes "black thread" on the list before pushing it across the table. She says, "I don't know," just as Boeta mumbles something, "On a broomstick" she thinks, but she isn't sure she heard right. She should say, "What was that?" Instead she takes Boeta's smooth freckled hand in her own and rests her head on the table, feeling the coarse grain against her cheek, the cool wood.

Postcards from November

Paisley

THE "S" AT THE END OF LES AND CARTES and postales is silent, I say, modulating my voice, hoping to conceal my dismay at Kate's terrible pronunciation. My fourteen-year-old's French oral exam is tomorrow and I want her to do well. She recently moved in with me after living with her father for six years. He must see I can care for her. I want him to let her stay.

We're seated at the dining-room table, surrounded by textbooks, a dictionary, her file stuffed with dog-eared handouts. I doodle an "s" on the notepad and cross it out, explain again about elision. In Afrikaans you pronounce everything you see. Nothing is hidden. It's a translucent language.

The paisley tablecloth is faded now. My mother bought it travelling in India. She went alone, to celebrate turning fifty. She took photographs of the Taj Mahal, the relics at Goa, the cripples.

I draw a clock face at three o'clock. My daughter fingers a pimple. I resist the urge to brush her hand away. Quelle heure est-il? I ask.

Trwuz urz, she says, rolling her eyes. I suppress a sigh and say, Nearly right. You pronounce the "s" at the end of trois because it connects to the "h" of heures, but the next "s" is silent. I used to teach music at l'École Française de Johannesbourg. Diplomats' kids, mostly, and contractors'.

Troubled souls who moved to new cities every few years, never settling anywhere.

I draw a clock face showing four o'clock.

Ma-ahm, she says, Gimme a break. All her friends have American accents. It's the fashion, learned on TV. We don't have one, but my daughter mimics her friends. TV's bad for your health, I'd said, when she asked. It makes you stupid. Still, she came to me. She said she wanted to live with her mom. She was tired of Jesus in the other house, and fellowship and worship blah blah.

Devons-nous faire une promenade? I say after an hour of conjugating verbs. She looks at me blankly. That means, Shall we go for a walk? Let's take a break.

We circle the park where small boys play cricket. Lightning flashes on the horizon. My daughter towers over me now, resting her arm on my shoulder momentarily. She's tall, like her grandmother. Her father sends her to a private college, a fancy place my parents couldn't have afforded.

When I fetch her from school, I'm to stay put in my little car. She doesn't want people noticing my shabby kit. I dressed up when I went to visit her teacher, wearing my crisp linen suit, with mascara applied and a lipstick called Sugarplum.

As we walk around the park, jacaranda blossoms pop underfoot, pungent explosions that turn to lilac sludge in the rain. Storm clouds have built, high and puffy, the sky black in the south. I've forgotten the French word for clouds, for thunder.

She says, Ma, Dad's driving me to Maritzburg this weekend. I want to go to boarding school. We're going to look at Epworth, at St John's. Good church schools.

Je t'enverrai une carte postale. I will send you a postcard.

The sun is low. The light reflecting off the clouds bounces against white security walls, blinding us. I reach out to her, to steady myself.

Crafty

Kate opens the fruit I bought from the Zimbabwean boy weaving between slow cars during rush hour. My window was down, even though it's a prime hijacking spot. The fan is broken, stuck on hot. Another boy tried selling us a beaded wire cow, big as a boot.

He said, Our mother in Harare, she make the crafty cows to feed hunger children.

We haven't space for clutter, but I pity them. They'll sleep next to the Braamfontein spruit if it doesn't rain, or in Hillbrow if it does. The river and the ghetto swallow children when they're raging.

The boys looked about Kate's age. I bought the bag of fruit, even though I knew the apples would be floury and the peaches dented. They'll be lucky if the police don't get them. The R20 I paid might keep them out of Lindela if they're caught.

At home, Kate asks, Can I give my baby a naartjie?

He'll love it, I say.

Won't be too acid?

He'll toss it if it is.

Her baby is a four-month-old Senegal parrot that bleats like a goat. Its eyes are still milky grey, its head round and fluffy. I bought the bird for her soon after she moved in with me, a manipulative device to try to hold her. Her father keeps cats. If she goes back to him, she'll have to leave the bird.

The day we returned from the pet shop, she hammered an old teaspoon, pinching the edges to form a spout for its open beak, which tugs like a nursing infant. He nibbles the orange peel, sneezing at the citrus vapour.

The phone rings. I freeze at the stove. Kate carries on peeling the naartjie with her long nails painted metallic green. Her father won't allow make-up. The phone rings a second time. We look at each other. My eyelids feel stuck in a too-wide stare.

It's probably him, she says, narrowing her eyes.

Let it ring, I say, my skin too tight, my lungs too small. We don't have caller ID.

Maybe it's an estate agent, she says, pragmatic, controlled.

I'll get it, I say, but she's already wiped her hands on her jeans and lifted the phone. Before answering she stares me down, reproaching, You gonna be scared all your days?

She says into the receiver, It's not a good time, Dad. We're making supper.

Kate moves into the passage, soothing him, saying, Don't worry. It's blown outta proportion. Call you later. Yeah.

After supper she rings him from her cell. I want to intervene, to stop her, to gesture a warning: be careful what you say. But I know I mustn't. I pretend I'm working on my computer, but I'm clicking keys so she won't notice I'm listening in.

Sos osss sos sis sssssss sos sos

I didn't want to worry you, she says.

asdfasdf lelelele ffff fuckufuckufuck

She says, We didn't keep you out the loop deliberately, to be spiteful.

llllooloo loo loop pool poopop pop

Last week's graffiti on the school toilet walls read: Kate Upton is a bulimic Satanist. That night, Kate swallowed six painkillers. She'd planned to swallow more but changed her mind and vomited them all up immediately.

Then she told me ten minutes later. I checked her colour, her pulse rate. Through the night, I listened to her breathe. I called the psychiatrist in the morning, setting up an appointment. I complained to the head teacher about the bullying, told her what had happened. The school told her father about the graffiti, the overdose. Then he phoned threatening: to take her away, to get a court order, to get the police involved.

She says, I'm fine, Dad, it'll be cool. Don't worry.

kkkkk llk llk lkjjkj kuku kook ok

Pi preens a strand of Kate's hair in his beak. She dyed it reddish-brown to match mine. I laughed, saying she'd need grey too if she wanted us to look snap-snap.

Yeah Dad, thanks Dad, she says, sounding American. The bird grooms her eyelashes. She dyed them too.

r re ref refu refuge refuge refugee eee eeeeeee

She laughs, and says, We wrote the Technology paper today. I had to design a wire cow, like the ones the Zimbos sell, you know, made of beads and wire. It wasn't great. I hadn't studied too well.

I want to shake her. She shouldn't say that. He'll blame me. He'll take you away.

zzz zim zimz babababa wee wee wee

She's quiet. Her father talks. She laughs again, saying, French on Monday.

oko oko kkkkk ok ok

Warning

We've been in the car for hours, Liz, driving the Mercedes, Madala, who sings haunting Zulu hymns, and me. We're travelling to Wits Rural, on the border of the Kruger Park. The light is falling over the dense thorn trees, and my earlier panic returns.

Today my ex drove her to Pietermaritzburg, to find a

boarding school. A place where she'll be safe, he'd said. A place away from me. I hope she hates the city, that she won't get a place. But maybe she's already romping through a lacrosse game with Enid Blyton, sharing a tuck box with Harry Potter.

I'm fantasising revenge on my return. Do I have the nerve to run my keys along his paintwork? Could I bribe the petrol joggie to "accidentally" put petrol in his diesel tank? Black mambas exist in this area. How hard is it to catch one? Could I turn a poisonous snake loose in his car boot one weekend when Kate's with me?

I ask Liz to stop by an abandoned farm stall. It rises, rusted ochre tin and broken glass, beside the road. I say I'm carsick, but it's not that. It's hate churning. I wish I could vomit out what I said last night when a helicopter wound overhead above our house, round and round. I said, I hope that helicopter is searching for the man who just murdered your father. Will I ever stop wounding my child?

We pass a welcome sign: Jesus Loves You, Hoedspruit Ministries. My tongue slithers over the ugly words forming. I should swallow them, but I spit: He's everywhere, isn't he? As soon as it's said, I'm ashamed, wishing it unsaid.

After arriving in the campsite, I'm taken to my bungalow. Madala points out the gap below the door. He's been here before. He says, Roll up a towel to wedge against the door. Tomorrow I'll show you the leopard spoor.

Bug Bites

We eat in the rondavel. Afterwards I check my teeth for lentils and spinach and, finding none, poke the black bubble on my gum between my lower front teeth. Pamela, our camp coordinator, cooks Sunshine Tart in the dark communal kitchen. What's in it? I ask. The table is sticky. I wish I had wine. Secret family recipe, she says.

It's delicious, tasting strongly of paprika, turmeric and mother-in-law's tongue, the only three spices in the store. The kitchen has mosquito nets for windows and we cook in turns. Everybody uses the same three spices for each meal. I'll be glad to cook in my own kitchen again. My table is properly clean; my kitchen cloths are washed and ironed. My own dishes sparkle and the sink hasn't got a permanently skuzzy ring.

At supper, I was glad of the dim globes hanging from the thatched roof because I couldn't rightly see what was beetle and what was sunshine in the pie. The fridge lists dangerously to one side, its door no longer closing properly. A notice taped on the freezer section warns residents to keep doors and windows closed. Monkeys and tree squirrels steal food.

If I had wine, I'd worry less about the mouse that ripped open the mealie meal or the dead snake on the road outside my bungalow. Perhaps its mate will be back to find it.

Another notice informs residents that this is a low-risk malaria area. It's the cool season now, rainy and humid, but not hot. I can't take the anti-malaria medicine. It makes me woozy and nauseous, and I can't think straight for weeks. The Dutch medical student, who is treating Aids patients at the hospital in Acornhoek, tells me it's probably safe. She says "day" for "they" and "dat" for "that". Her voice swoops and bounces like the buck that scampers for cover when disturbed. I want to listen to her talk forever, but when we hear the hoo-whoop hoo-whoop of the hyena, everyone falls silent, listening in awe.

Before leaving for camp, I saw a dentist. He said the bubble on my gum was not a malignant tumour, just a blood blister, caused by plaque calcified between my teeth. Flossing would dislodge the plaque, and the blister would burst and disappear.

I scratch the red welt on my ankle where I slapped a mosquito. It left a bloody smear. I hope the Dutch girl is right.

Management of Snake Bite

1) *Allay the patient's anxiety. Stay as calm as possible.*

   The ground in the camp is dusty, but the trees are green. The tags identifying them in Latin have rusted, and I don't know their English names. The birdcalls are unfamiliar too, sounding like hammers on anvils or rusted hinges. They rasp and grate. My daughter said I must be on the lookout for the yellow-billed hornbill. She said they studied it at school. An insect flies into my eye. I wash it out with saline from the Dutch medic. I can't be bothered to read the bird book after that. My eye keeps watering. I ignore the bird search.

2) *Shock can be more toxic than the bite itself. Deaths have been reported where patients have been bitten by harmless snakes.*

   At 9am, I wind along the road towards the camp's exit under a hazy sky, wearing sunglasses. My windows are closed but dust swirls though the air vent, along with dried seed husks, dead beetles, shards of twig and grass. I snap the vents shut, then cross the dry riverbed where snakes catch frogs. I've seen the little pop-eyed frogs at my door, nearly stepped on one in the dark.

3) *Not all snakes are poisonous.*

   The gap below the door to my rondavel is big enough to let through a snake, but not a frog. Before I enter, I rattle the doorknob, jiggle the door. I'm scared to look under my bed. Before I put my shoes on in the morning, I shake them out. I even check the gloves of the potholder in the kitchen, in case something has

81

fallen from the grass roof. This wariness feels like being married again.

4) *Not all poisonous snakes are fully charged with venom.*

I drive in second gear, watching for buck among the thorn trees, afraid one might leap out. On the road outside the camp, I plug my earphones in, dial my iPod looking down and then speed up. I want to listen to something calming. When I look up again, the road is curving sharply. A cow is meandering across the road. It's too late to brake; I speed up, swerving around it. Just beyond, I pull over, shaking, sweating. *The Cell Block Tango* from *Chicago* pipes through the earphone:

He had it coming. He had it coming. He only had himself to blame.

If you'd a been there. If you'd a seen it. I betcha you would a done the same!

5) *Even snakes fully charged with venom do not always inject a lethal dose.*

I recognise the trees and flowers that grow beside the public buildings as I drive into Hoedspruit: poinsettia, jacaranda, canna and frangipani, their heady scents, the violently coloured flowers with poisonous milk that flow from their stems when picked. They grew in our Pinetown garden when I was a child. There were green mambas in those trees too. I watched the gardener kill one once. It writhed for hours after he'd decapitated it with a panga.

6) *Reassurance lowers blood pressure, reducing palpitations, tremors, sweating and rapid breathing, hence reducing the speed of absorption of toxins.*

We sit, my friends and I, on their patio overlooking the bush, sipping lemonade. They're the new doctors in town, a husband-and-wife team from Joburg. He does the general practice; she does the pathology and women's medicine. He asks about my eye. I dismiss it. Let me look, he says. I turn to him, he holds open my eyelid. It's infected already, he says. If it's not better by tomorrow, come in to the practice. I'll set you up with antibiotic drops.

7) *Some patients get infections or allergic reactions from so-called harmless snakes.*

On the way back to the camp I drive slower, mindful of cows. My ex calls. His initials flash on the cell phone. I don't want to answer, but I'm too afraid not to. He's in Pietermaritzburg looking at church schools. He says, Don't shoot me, I'm just the messenger. Kate asked me to call you. She's sitting right here. She wants me to tell you that she's really terrified of you. She says you make her feel guilty about wanting to go to boarding school. Now I'm just the messenger, remember...

I click off the phone and pull over, just before Jesus Loves You. I slump over the wheel, sobbing.

Waterhole

I fill up at the Blyde River fuel station, the same place I stopped three days ago when I went to interview Andries, the excavator operator up at Mariepskop. The pungent odour of petrol is a jolt. It reminds me of my father teaching me to drive, instructing me to pull up on the same side as the gas tank. There's only a bottle store here, the plant-hire place and a kafee.

I ask after Upside-down Thomas, who'd filled my tank earlier in the week. The attendant shrugs. I'm relieved, just making small talk. Upside-down Thomas had told me he was studying Public Relations through correspondence. He asked me for a job, asked me to help him. Gee, I said feeling like a culprit, I wish I could. Jobs are hard to find.

I'd printed the cheque with my fountain pen. Thomas

had admired the pen, but it felt like an accusation. When I blew on the wet ink, he narrowed his eyes below his black-and-blue peak. I figured his studies were a fiction. He held my cheque, looking long and hard at my name, pulling on the paper, stroking it between his fingers.

I'd said, Keep up your studies, Thomas. I hope you get lucky soon. On the job front, I added, blushing.

I'll try my level best, he'd answered, licking his lips.

I buy bottled water at the kafee and walk back, swinging my packet, singing, happy to be going home. I'd spent the week on assignments for the magazine, interviewing vehicle operators for the transport issue, talking to local business owners. I've missed my daughter.

There were monkeys, a hornbill, an eagle and lots of different buck. I saw the large holes dug by warthog undermining the electric fences, and the spoor of big cats. I saw a snake that left no trail in the gravel, so that after it had gone, I doubted I'd seen it. It was hot at the campsite and the river had dried up. The tap water had tasted soapy.

I feel dehydrated, glad of the sparkling mineral water I like so much. I unscrew the lid, loving the hiss, anticipating the first sharp mouthful.

The garage owner in Kamogelo told me he used to have two excellent mechanics, but one just up and died. The one I interviewed didn't look too good, either. He was thin, with yellowed eyes and lesions on his skull. The mechanic has to train somebody new soon, but the problem with that, he'd said, is that the new guy is going to up and die on you too. It's tricky.

The owner of the plant-hire company rents out earth-moving equipment to farmers building dams. He can't employ his men over weekends, can't keep his equipment operating enough hours in the month to pay off his bank loan. He has to let them go Saturdays, for funerals. Every week, another funeral. They're croaking like frogs, he'd said. You know the end is near when they start sleeping every tea break and lunch hour, napping on the ground if there's a twenty-minute wait.

While I'm waiting for the cash slip, a man at the next pump greets me like he knows me. I don't remember him. Thomas? I ask, tentative. No, he says, Goodenough.

Good to see you, Goodenough, I say, confused. Perhaps I interviewed his colleague, the mechanic, or the forklift driver. Was he a friend of the excavator operator? I can't place him.

You go where?

Home, I say, Jozi, taking just a sip from the water bottle, but wanting to guzzle.

Jozi's a big city, he says, watching my throat. I don't know anyone there.

It's a big city, I say, dabbing my lips.

A man needs a friend in Jozi, he says, still staring at my throat. My knees turn to paste. Perhaps you give me your number, he says.

Perhaps I don't, I say, looking at the gravel that yields no footprints.

Clip

My daughter lies on her stomach on the wooden floor. Her legs are under my bed. She points my camera at her baby parrot, which is holding a grape in its bandaged foot. I bought grapes and mangoes and avocado pears at a wooden stall near the Blyde River yesterday.

Why's Pi eating in my room? I ask, staring at the beard of pulp around his beak. He shakes his head and the mush disperses across the parquet tiles.

He likes the décor, says Kate.

You mean he can see the floor in here, I say, wiping up grape particles with a tissue.

Whaddevah, she says. A flash. Light bounces off the walls, my wardrobe. Gotcha!

We've been apart for five days, me in the bush, her looking at boarding schools with her father. Her pet had stayed at the vet because it needed antibiotics. We left Karma, the other bird, the one that had ripped out Pi's claw, with a friend.

Clean up after him when you're done, I say. I don't want to tread in sticky stuff.

She ignores me.

She had constructed a toy for his cage, looping together old keys, a dead tin opener, a plastic toy, and the silver ring I gave her last birthday. She'd worried about him being fretful. The toy will distract him, she'd said.

Don't let him chew the electrics, I say.

You hear that, Pi? No wires for nibblies. Don't want a Fried Pi. No burned beak. What would the vet say? Abusive parents, neglectful mothers. Pass a tissue, Ma.

I hand her the box. She wipes the bird's face. It struggles. Stop fussing, Pi baby.

Take one of me and Pi, Mom. I click. We laugh. She reviews the images, showing them to the bird on her shoulder. Look, that's you, Pi. You're cute. And photogenic. She holds the image out to me. He says it's a bad pic. The angle's not right. He's looking away.

Take another, Mom. I'll need good photos of me and Pi. For my wall. At boarding school.

Crest

I'm ten minutes early at the psychologist's rooms where the mediation is being held. Kate's father is there already, talking to his lawyer, whose mascara is punishing. I hold out my hand. Her fingers are sticks, her handshake pointed, hurting.

I'm wearing my black work skirt, ironed, the mauve silk jacket I bought at a second-hand shop for its good label. The heels do it, make me look competent, perhaps even pretty.

Her father returns to his car, retrieving a folder from the boot. The last jacaranda blossoms fall on the roof. I say to the lawyer, Did he tell you today was the day? She scrutinises me as if she's hearing-impaired. It's too late to stop the story. I say, Twenty-one years ago today, we got married.

She says, No, he didn't tell me that.

I feel an idiot. But I'm not finished. I say, I was nineteen.

He returns and rings the doorbell. While we wait, a woman in the street answers her cell phone. She talks loudly, saying, That wasn't the deal; I can't possibly agree. She's big, with cropped hair, wearing quilted salmon. From the way she opens her car door, I know she's unafraid.

I carry my laptop in a briefcase. Moral support – that self I'm still proud of: photographer, writer. Digital codes more real than paper, than court orders.

Inside is dark and cool. A dragonfly hovers above a decorative koi pond at the entrance. This is going to be an expensive two hours. I'll pay the child psychologist; he'll pay the lawyer.

They open their folders, take notes when I talk, and say things like, Let me remind you… find a way forward… in the child's best interest… appropriate developmental stage… manipulation.

The lawyer tells me I'm still playing the victim game, but I don't listen too closely because my daughter has changed her mind, doesn't want to go to boarding school after all.

I'm not sorry her father found out about her overdose from the school. I'm glad he was humiliated. I don't say so, don't need to. I am sorry I said terrible things about him to my daughter. I promise not to do it again, not because they're extracting the words from me, but because I made her cry. Mostly I'm relieved that the fight's gone out of this thing, because nobody can make a fourteen-year-old do what she doesn't want to do. No judge in the land. That's what the lawyer says.

I study a framed print of Beethoven's ear on the wall. Was he still alive when they sloshed his head in blue paint, lying him sideways on the canvas? Was he already deaf? Already dead?

The notes of a symphony wander along the edge of his cheek, superimposed in silver. Strings of quavers crest the helix and anti-helix, twirl about his earlobe, and march out toward the frame.

Words

Check these five words, I say. Kate takes the page in one hand, looking closer, holding a banana smoothie. Yam or yarn, she says. I'm doing a word puzzle, a linguistic charade. Three letters, I say.

She looks at the next clue, says, What about horn? Horn-rimmed spectacles, maybe? A trumpet, a vuvuzela?

In America, a hooter is a horn, I say.

Hooters in America, she says with theatrical flair, are tits. You'd know this if you had a Facebook page.

I would?

She nods and hands me the paper as she climbs under the white embroidered cover into bed with me, her bird on her shoulder. Has Pi had a crap lately? I ask.

Yes, she says, irritated. You think I'm not a good mother? Pi thinks so too.

I say, Why would I think that? Why would he?

He's making a funny noise, like, not a happy noise, just cross, growling. When she turns to kiss the bird, it squeaks. See? Like that.

Pi is hungry, I say. Put him in his cage to eat. I don't want him spoiling my bedclothes.

Ma-ahm. He's not hungry. I already fed him a grape.

Shall we get back to the words? She picks at the pilling on her acid-green socks, the same colour as the bird, flicking them onto the coverlet. I stop myself from telling her not to. She tells me that when fabrics are washed incorrectly, the fibres get tangled, like hairballs. We learned about it in Home Economics. Clearly you don't wash my socks properly.

Is that right?

The bird screeches in her ear, she pulls away, wincing, laughing. She looks at him, asks, Why you growling, Pi?

He's telling you to wash your own socks. Now take him to his cage.

But, she says, petulantly, I want him to stay with me; I want him to be happy on my shoulder.

Oh?

She'd screamed at me when I told her no boarding school. You're so selfish. You're supposed to put my needs ahead of your own. Her father had told her I was disturbed. It's not normal for adults to need their teenage kids like your mother does.

So, she says, scratching the translucent skin beneath Pi's beak. She looks at me sideways. Maybe I'm doing the same bloody horrible thing you do. She smirks at the hairpin logic.

I return to my puzzle. In America a hooter is a horn. Or a tit.

Tangle

It's Kate's last day of the school year. She's dyed her hair again. The towels and tiles and shower curtain are smudged with dark inky stains. I thought she'd go orange when her roots started showing, or red, but no. Black.

We talked about losing the Satanist look, giving up the pentagram she wears on a chain round her neck, ditching the book of teenage witch spells. I raised my eyebrows when she emerged from the shower, her hair a wet mess of clinging black snakes.

Tonight, I'll take her to her father for the Christmas holidays. She'll sling her kit in the boot. I'll kiss her and her bird. She's taking it along. Her father has erected a hook in the courtyard where she can hang the cage, safe from the cats.

I am writing up the article on the excavator operator I interviewed in Limpopo last week. There's just time before we leave to phone the plant-hire business owner who drove me to the farm. He is a white Zimbabwean who lost his farm in the land invasions. I ask him the details I forgot to write down at the time: the make of the vehicle, the tonnage, the names of the butterflies he'd pointed out.

Kate starts up the hairdryer in my bedroom. I put my hand over the receiver, saying, Can't you go do that someplace else? She switches the hairdryer off, but doesn't leave.

The plant-hire guy had showed me a green-banded swallowtail, a glossy black butterfly with a strip of emerald green on its wings, and a giant white one, clouded mother-of-pearl. We also saw a shy impala ram that bounded away before I could take a photograph. He told me it was a conservancy, where endangered species are protected.

Kate preens in the mirror, stretching her neck, swinging her head, spraying the glass.

I ask, How is the repair to the dam going? How is Andries?

Not well, he says. He has shingles. I guess he'll join the sleepers soon.

Hey, I say, I'm so sorry.

Kate stares close to the mirror at her new black eyebrows, making wide eyes.

Hey, he says. You take care.

Ride the
Tortoise

MY LEFT BREAST IS COOL AND PALE. The right is shiny and red, a furious apple. The nipple has disappeared, so the baby can't latch when I lift my shirt and try to feed him, sitting in the front passenger seat of the car. His fists pummel my unyielding flesh. He nuzzles the other side, but it's empty, hasn't filled up since his last unsatisfactory feeding. I jiggle him up and down until he falls asleep to a tenor singing Mahler's *Kindertotenliede* on the CD player. My husband says I must put him back in the car seat, for safety reasons. He reads aloud in snatches from the guide book balanced on the steering wheel.

Covering much of the central Namib Desert and the Naukluft Mountains, the Namib Naukluft Park is home to some of the rarest and weirdest plant and animal species in the world.

I don't want to put the baby back in his car seat. He'll wake because he's still hungry, and there isn't another car in sight. We haven't passed anything but stones on this ruler-straight road for two hours. My husband will insist though, telling me it's the rule of the road, the law. He's the driver. He'll say he doesn't want to argue with South West Afri… he'll correct himself, Namibian traffic cops. He's not going to languish in foreign jails on account of my refusing to strap the bloody baby in. I want him to stop the car so I can get out and return the baby to the car seat more easily, so I can get a drink from the cooler in the boot. If I ask, he'll say he doesn't want to stop unnecessarily, will demand to know why I can't just stretch through the seats.

I should try to reason with him. I should say, Yes, dear, there are many things we don't want to stop unnecessarily, like me playing the contrabassoon in the orchestra for the last symphony season. I had to stop. For the baby. Some things we must do for the little ones. The low vibrations of the instrument shook right through my belly to loosen the lining of my womb. I didn't know I was in premature labour. I hadn't wanted to interrupt the maestro unnecessarily in the middle of the symphony concert.

Everything was fine once I got home and lay on my bed. For a while. I hadn't wanted to disturb the doctor in the middle of the night with my aching back. An aching back is normal in pregnancy. I'd thought I was imagining things when the weak contractions began twelve weeks early.

I should say, Please stop. He's getting too heavy. It hurts my back to twist and lift.

The baby wakes a little later and his crying starts my milk again. I lift my shirt and a small spray escapes onto the dashboard. I cover the flow quickly, but it drips on the seat. My husband swerves to a stop, dabbing the dashboard with a handkerchief. "Get out," he says, "I don't want a sticky mess."

My daughter sucks her thumb. "My baby is crying too," she says. "Dolly wants milk. Wash waah waah." The doll, the tenor and the baby chant a bizarre desert counterpoint. Brahms' *Lullaby* would have been a better choice than this lament for all the dead infants of the earth. Poor Mahler, poor Mrs Mahler who lost their child to scarlet fever.

I stand beside the crimson Audi, refusing to cry as I knead my recalcitrant breast, waiting for it to burst and flow. The telephone poles along the road stretch from Helmeringhausen to Sesriem, miles of dust and low thorn bushes. We're travelling through the Maltehöhe region. Our destination is the Duwisib Castle. This morning we left the mineral springs at Ai-Ais.

The mineral springs were rumoured to have healing properties for arthritis, lung complaints and nervous disorders.

Milk from the good breast spurts in a pale arc onto the hot tar, where it turns to steam. I wish it were feeding my boy, but the blockage on the other side won't budge. After a while, the spurting arc turns into a dribble, falling on my shoes. When it dries, it will linger, tacky on my skin. My husband adjusts the volume on the car stereo to drown out the hungry screams.

"Nun will die Sonn' so hell aufgehn…" sings the soloist over marching violins. *Now the sun will rise as brightly as if no misfortune had occurred in the night.*

I steady myself on the wing mirror, holding only the frame so as not to leave fingerprints on the glass. The telephone poles disappear into the pink mountains in one direction and into the desert in the other. How long will my husband wait? He turns the music up a little more. He does that when he's irritated. Once, back at home, before we had children, he got tired of waiting for me, so he drove off without me. I took too long, he said later, after I arrived at the party in a taxi.

If he drives away now, will he leave the children with me? Maybe he'll drive off, to scare me, as a joke. If he takes the children, it won't be funny. Will I plod from pole to pole? I press my breast and listen to the voices sparking along the drooping cable.

"Sind Sie dort?" *Are you there?* "Ich bin night hier!" The voices whisper: I am not here. Where are you? There's no one here.

If I can hold out to the castle, there must surely be a hot shower, but if he leaves me, will I crumple and stop breathing, or will I crawl, dragging my nipples through the desert sand?

The telephone poles watch me massage that plug. It must work its way out soon, so that the baby can latch again. I press and press, but nothing happens. I twist my nipple hoping to roll the blockage out, wanting to scream at the pain, not wanting to scare my little girl rocking in her car seat, with her fingers in her ears. She also does not like Mahler.

When I get back in the car, my husband reads aloud from the map:

The Castle lies 1475 metres above sea level, and its geographical co-ordinates are 25° 15' 48" South and 16° 32' 40" East.

The whole journey has been an expensive trip undertaken in a bid to get to know each other again. Eight months after my baby's arrival, my husband wants the bedroom back to normal.

"When we get home," he says, "the baby can go on the bottle; he'll sleep in the cot in the next room." I will offer my breasts to my husband instead. He thinks it's a good idea if I go back to work and play in the orchestra again. "It will be nice for you," he says. "It's not a big job, after all, to play the contrabassoon. Mostly you just sit and wait, play a few long notes here and there and go home again afterwards. It will get you out of the house a bit, give you something to do. It's good for a woman to have her own interests."

Dead Vlei is a vast dent of dry, compacted clay dotted with the ghostly figures of ancient camel thorn trees, preserved by the heat and dry air.

The trip is supposed to accomplish all this. We've driven 7000 kilometres hardly speaking to each other – a silence untouched by crying children and the weight of Mahler, punctuated only by comments he's shared from the guide book.

95

The San people used the milky latex produced by Euphorbia to prepare their poisoned hunting arrows and also to poison water holes.

The noise in my head gathers again, layers of sounds, the low moan of the dunes, a weeping *Welwitchia mirabilis*, the stones on the grumbling hills that mutter and hiss a dark percussion. And Mahler, always adding his sorrow. I hope the shower cubicle in the place where we are going will have a sharp tiled edge, so I might bang my head under very hot water to drown out the clamour.

We arrive early in the afternoon. The wind has an icy edge. There is a shower in a vast cool bathroom, but only a feeble trickle emerges from the rattling pipe. My skin is gooseflesh and my nipples contract. I press the thickened spot and massage downward under the tepid water, toward the nipple, like the clinic sister showed me. My hard breast will not ooze a single milky tear.

Last time the duct was blocked, I stood under the shower and massaged my breast, stroking downwards, over and over. The noise in my head got louder, like piccolos warming up, joined by a sax, an oboe and then a hundred violins, each tuning to a different pitch. I had to get the plug out. I turned the water up, hotter, until it scalded my skin. Eventually the blockage burst from my nipple and pinged against the glass door. The release was instant. A solid jet of milk drummed against the tiles and a blue-white swirl flowed down the drain. My head was finally still.

But this shower has just a shallow rim of bricks with a plastic curtain that hangs from a sagging rail. I bang my head on the outermost wall, next to the window, on the other side of the bungalow from where my husband minds the babies. I flush the toilet to mask the sound, but the ritual is incomplete and unsatisfying. Without hot water, without the sharp edge, there can be no purge of breast or brain in this alien spot.

My husband calls through the bathroom door, urges me to hurry. The scheduled tour of the castle begins in twenty minutes. We didn't come all this way to miss it. I need a hot compress. If only I could soak a towel and microwave it – but there is no electricity. I keep forgetting. I look for a hot water bottle. I could heat a kettle on the gas flame. Could I put a soaked towel in the gas oven? My throbbing breast must wait until after the tour.

"The castle was built by Baron Captain Heinrich von Wolf in 1909," says the tour guide, who has no lips. I stare at the vast chandelier in the abandoned castle. My husband compares what the tour guide says with the notes in his brochure. "The Baron returned to Dresden after the Nama-Herero uprising and married the stepdaughter of the US consul."

The chandelier begins to vibrate. Nobody else notices. It is the beating of the Baron's heart that still echoes in the castle's twenty-two empty rooms. When I ask the tour guide if it beats with hope or horror, my husband says, "Now, now, that will do." He asks the tour guide about the severe oil portraits hanging on the wall. Who was the artist? When were they painted?

"The Baron and his wife," says the guide as we continue into the next room, "commissioned an architect to build the castle. He wanted it to reflect his commitment to the German military cause. The building materials were imported from Germany, and travelled 600 kilometres by ox-wagons after landing at Lüderitz."

My daughter wants to feed the tortoise the Baron left behind. I am scared it will bite off her hand. It is a vengeful giant, angry at being abandoned. The tour guide says the tortoise is four hundred years old. I watch its ancient eyes. They have a rabid look.

My husband braais under a black sky hung with an infinitude of crystal drops. After dinner, we watch shooting stars. My heart beats like the Baron's and I know that one hundred feral horses are galloping toward us both, the Baron and me. The Baron strolls over to our stoep and pulls up a chair, asking us to please excuse his shabby attire. "I've been at war," he says. We drink a Meerlust Cabernet under the stars. It tempers the cold night air. The baby niggles at the good breast. My daughter wants to watch TV. She doesn't like strangers and wants to go inside, to watch Teletubbies or Barney. I explain that television doesn't work on gas. She wants Smarties. She wants to go home. She cries herself to sleep in a lumpy bed with a scratchy woollen blanket.

I try again after the Baron has left, to help my son latch onto my swollen breast after he's emptied the other one. He cries and cries in the wavery gaslight. I jiggle him on my hip, rubbing my fingers over his gums. I recite the names of the regions of Namibia: Caprivi, Erongo, Hardap, Karas, Okavango, Khomas, Kunene, Ohangwena, Omaheke, Omusati, Oshana, Oshikoto, Otjozondjupa.

The baby has a fever. I knock the bottle of mint-green medicine over in the dark. The spill is sticky in my slippers. I recite the names of the German settlers who left their boldly coloured homes dotted around the desert, with pointed roofs, so the snow wouldn't accumulate on their balconies and turrets. They should have stayed at home with Herr Heckel and Herr Püchner and Herr Mollenhauer, who fashioned bocals and bells for bassoons instead.

At 2am, the croup starts. Babies die from that – even back in Joburg, at Morningside Clinic, with paediatricians and oxygen tents. I try to boil the kettle over the gas stove, but it makes a puny wisp of steam. The kitchen is cold. I don't know what to do. I remember the telephone poles and want to call my mother. She would tell me to keep the baby upright. I sit him in my arms, to keep him from crying, to keep his airways open. I recite the list of composers who wrote studies for the bassoon: Giampieri, Milde, Orefici, Oubradous, Ozi, Piard, Pivonka, Weissenborn.

The tour guide had spoken in a voice that sounded like snakes winding across the desert, telling of stonemasons from Italy, Switzerland and Ireland, hired to build the castle. Did they leave their wives and babies at home with their violins and tambourines? Am I the first woman to nurse a sick child at this castle? Were there even any ghosts here to tell me what to do?

The tour guide had told, in a voice that sounded like thorn trees rattling in the wind, of how the First World War broke out while the Baron was travelling to Europe in 1914. The ship carrying him and his wife was diverted to Rio. Lush Rio, warm Rio, Rio of hot sand and sultry beaches, bananas and guavas, melons and pawpaw. Oh Baron, why didn't you take me with you when you left this barren spot? Come back for me, come back for my babies.

At 3am, I call a doctor 150 kilometres away. He says, "Ja, you know that Jayta, the Baron's wife, has found passage to Europe on a Dutch ship, and the Baron is disguised as a woman to avoid arrest. On arrival in Europe, the Baron is scheduled to rejoin the German army."

"So what must I do, Herr Doktor?"

"Keep the baby on the breast and disguise yourself as a man," he says. "I'll see you in the morning at my rooms."

"How will I get there?"

"Make a plan."

At 4am, I call the maestro, to ask him to perform the last rites telephonically. He says, "I am occupied on the battlefield of the Somme, giving the last rites to soldiers dying in the mud. The noise inside your head is bothering me."

"There's no sharp edge in this shower and flat walls don't help," I say.

"Make a plan," he says. "How can I perform my spiritual duty when you're making such a din?"

I want to tie my baby on my back and creep through the dark, over the rocky ground back to the castle. I want to find the armoire where the antique weapons are stored, but the Baron has returned and blocks the door. He refuses to let me pass.

"Was wollen Sie?" he asks, ushering me back to bed.

I want a gun. It seems a good idea under difficult circumstances. "Ich brauche ein Gewehr," I say, unaware I can speak German. I didn't know the word for "gun" was "gewehr". Or have I forgotten?

"Haben Sie ein Gewehr?" he asks.

I do not have a gun. He tells me I should do my wifely duty. I say the trip isn't practical. Not with a baby and a toddler. We should have stayed home. The castle could have waited. A sound begins like a flock of birds landing on the roof.

"Wife, do your duty."

I tell him it's not practical to play the contrabassoon any more. The reeds are too hard, the instrument too heavy. I do not like to play it. I do not want to perform. The sound is the rattling spiccato of poisoned arrows shaking in a quiver.

"Put the child down. You must obey."

I tell him the child is sick; I must keep him upright. The baron finally hears the sound and says, "My horses, my horses. They're returning to the stables." But horses don't sound like pebbles on glass. He crosses to the window and casts open the curtains. By the starlight glinting off his buttons and buckle, a many-armed brown woman enters, riding the tortoise. She takes off her shoes, revealing the feet of a girl.

At first I think she's a Teutonic Kali, who will wrap my legs around the Baron's neck and show me how to bite off his head. I say, "Kali, Kali, will you lift up my chin and guide my teeth? I've never done this before. Please teach me how to drink his blood."

"Hush, hush," says the woman, wiping my brow. She blows on coals in an ancient pot and sprinkles herbs that flare and sizzle.

I say, "Kali, Kali, bring me those guns, one in each hand: for my daughter, for my son; one in my mouth, one thrust between my legs."

"Hush, hush," says the woman, taking my baby in two wrinkled arms. She rocks and holds him, a hot pack to his chest. A swirl of eucalyptus scents the room, moistened air frizzes his hair.

"Hush, hush," says the woman, as two arms, their skin neither young, nor yet crepey, unbutton my pyjamas. She lifts my red-streaked breast in one hand, holding a warm poultice to my burning skin. The air smells of mustard and bitter yearning. The baby sneezes, saying, "Bless you."

The many-armed brown woman slices open the spiked leaf of an aloe, scrapes its glistening gel and smears it on my breast. She massages it down from my armpit in small circular motions, blowing on the hot spot and talking to the tortoise; pulling and kneading with her fingertips until the plug breaks free.

The milk jets onto the hot coals and hisses a fragrant cloud of steam, "Sie sind nicht allein." The baby sneezes again. "Bless you."

Signs from
the Kitchen

Speed Bumps Ahead

I WAS ABOUT TO PUT THE ROAST in the oven so it would be done on our return from church, when the phone rang. The chicken was stuffed and sprinkled with white wine and rosemary. The carrots, potatoes and onions were in the roasting pan. I opened the oven door, slid the pan in, then dried my hands on a clean dishtowel and brushed some hair from my eyes.

It would be my sister in Sydney riding out the last of her weekend. When I finally answered, I'd hear the usual litany: she was depressed and homesick and drunk; she was blocked, unable to complete her novel because she had too little contact with her kids; she was sick of her ex pressuring her to return to rehab for a non-existent problem; she was broke and couldn't fly back to Joburg, which would be cheaper than rehab, and more useful.

I asked our eldest to change the baby's nappy, yelled at the middle two to brush their teeth, and stepped around the black cat with the bracelet of white fur that was rubbing against me. My sister wouldn't remember that we were heading to worship. She'd need sympathy, and wouldn't want to say goodbye.

If I answered, my husband would come into the kitchen, cock his head at the phone and jingle his car keys. I'd mouth, okay, I'm coming. He did server duty and wanted to arrive early to supervise the altar boys. I'd have to keep it short, try not to sound impatient when I picked up the receiver. I'd promise to call her tomorrow, staying up till midnight to call her back. If I were snippy, she'd cry. It would take an extra ten minutes to get off the phone.

It often happened like this. Once I'd finally shaken her loose, we'd race to church, my husband hurling the car at the speed bumps, jolting us all to arrive on time. I'd cover my eyes to keep from panicking. The kids would smack and pinch in the back. We'd arrive with someone crying, someone sulking, and me clammy and gasping.

The phone rang off before I answered. Odd, I thought. She never did that. She'd let it ring for an hour if she wanted to talk. Who else would call so early on a Sunday?

I wiped the counter; the phone rang again. I answered on the first ring. It was my sister's ex-husband, sorry, bad news from the hospital. He'd known something was wrong because my sister wouldn't answer her phone. The cops broke down her door. After overdosing on sleeping tablets and cough syrup and Jack Daniels, she'd inhaled her own vomit.

He said he was at her bedside in the ICU. She hasn't got long, he said. She's brain dead. My husband walked in and jingled the car keys at me and tapped his watch. I nodded. My sister's ex wanted to give me a chance to say goodbye, offered to hold the cell phone to her ear, so I could say a few words. I couldn't think of a thing to say.

Hairpin Bend

I was about to put the fish in the oven because it was finally hot enough. The oven is old, like me, and takes its own sweet time. When it was ready, I couldn't remember where I'd put the fish. I looked all over the house – in the hall where I came in, in the passage where I paused to switch on the light, in the bathroom where I stopped on my way to the kitchen to relieve myself. I even checked my bedroom cupboard, in case I'd left it there when I put away my boots.

Memory is fickle at 75, but I know I bought that fish. I'm sunburned from waiting in a queue for it at the open-air market in Kalk Bay, and my hair got blown about in the wind. I know I brought it home because after I got off the train, the packet I carried it in banged against my leg, feeling cool through the newspaper. I checked to make sure the cheese I'd bought wasn't packed up against the fish, getting contaminated.

I can still recite all the saints and martyrs in Latin: Petri et Pauli, Andreae, Jacobi, Joannis, Thomae, Jacobi, Philippi, Bartholomaei, Matthaei, Simonis, et Thaddaei: Lini, Cleti, Clementis, Xysti, Cornelii, Cypriani, Laurentii, Chrysogoni, Joannis et Pauli, Cosmae et Damiani, et omnium Sanctorum tuorum.

I'm sure I dressed the fish in lemon and garlic because the lemon has been cut and is lying on the counter. My hands smell of garlic. Am I remembering how I prepared another fish on another day?

Deponent verbs use active conjugations for tenses that do not exist in the passive: the gerund, the supine, the present and future participles and the future infinitive. But I cannot remember what I did with the fish.

My grandsons are coming for supper. We always eat fish on Friday. Once it's nearly done and I'm chopping the feta cheese into the salad, I send them down to buy the chips from Saleem's. I can't be boiling great pots of oil with my arthritic claws. When the buzzer at the entrance beeps, they'll bound up the stairs laughing and smelling of sea and salt and vinegar.

I can still construct a decent contract, or draft an eloquent opinion or addendum, or find some obscure proviso to protect a client. That knowledge swims to the front of my mind when I call it up.

But, when I phone my daughter to tell her that I've lost the fish, I forget why I called. I ask her instead what time the boys will arrive. She says, no Ma, they're not coming. They're at varsity, in Grahamstown. She says, what day of the week is it, Ma? And then I know it isn't Friday. She says, it's Sunday, Ma, didn't you go to Mass today?

Traffic Circle

I was about to put the mixture in the oven when I remembered I'd forgotten to include the eight eggs the double-batch recipe called for. My new pink pyjamas were spattered with brownie batter. I was taking dessert to a distant relative's housewarming, some place near Pretoria. My cousin said she expected forty people. I needed a lot of brownies.

Scraping the mixture back in the bowl, I discovered there weren't enough eggs. As a statement telling my children that I really do care for them, this stunt looked doomed. They've asked for homemade brownies, grumbling that I'm never available, always at the computer.

When the beeper went off, I pulled the tray out and dipped a knife in to check its doneness. Soggy dough stuck to the tip. It was raw in the middle, but black at the edge.

It was too late to bake another batch. Already half an hour late for the bring-and-share, I printed the email with directions before we left, smudging the still-wet ink as I tugged it from the printer.

Take Botha Ave off-ramp. Right @ lights. Left @ T-junction end of Botha.

My husband drove along a narrow road through the town, looking for the T-junction. I couldn't help nodding off. I'd worked too late, been up too early. What's the next landmark? I asked, checking that he'd been listening to me. He looked vague. The children sniggered in the back. A sign to a train station appeared round the next bend. Am I looking for the station? he asked. No, I said through gritted teeth, you're looking for a T-junction.

I dozed off again. On waking, there was a sign to Olifantsfontein. No T-junction? I asked. No T-junction, he said. No T-junction, said the kids. We watched while you slept.

It was 10 kilometres to the next town. We were two hours late. Beside the road was a rough gravel verge. No handy lay-by where we could pull off, just the railway line and the long grass beyond.

If we retraced our route, the leftover meat at the party would have shrivelled to hunks of tepid biltong, the salads withered with the stilted conversation.

My husband pulled over beside a lonesome eucalyptus with a stunted spine. Perhaps we should drive on to the next town, find a Wimpy, and call in our apologies tomorrow, I said.

My husband said nothing. I wanted to sleep. I needed to get back to my work. My daughter unsealed the Tupperware container, now sticky with age, and bit into a burnt brownie. I can't wait, she said. My son took one too. Mom, he said, this tastes like shit. He stepped out the car and spat into the dust. Then he flung the brownie in an arc over the silent railway line.

No Stopping

I was about to put the rusks in the oven to dry out at a low temperature, when the donkey brayed at the open door. It gave me such a fright I dropped the tray and the crumbly squares scattered all over the floor. Sjoe! I was cross. The farmer likes my rusks best of all. He says they're the best rusks in the whole of the Koue Bokkeveld, better even than his wife's.

Jissie en katiepie! I screamed at my bloody fool son, still sleeping in the next room. Probably didn't tether the donkey properly when he rolled in last night, drunk out of his tree. Payday is a piss-up every month.

Outside, the poor beast stood with the cart still attached, driven right through the vegetable patch. The lettuces are crushed, the tomatoes ruined, the beans ripped from the stakes and tangled in the cart's wheels. I pull a stake from the ground. The earth is weeping, the donkey brays. I lead the beast to the water trough and unhitch the cart.

My son comes out in a trance, blinking in the light, clutching his head. Payday, you bliksem, has only just begun, I scream. I'm going to beat you till your bones are broken, till your blood spurts across the sky. I'm not stopping until the farmer comes over and grabs this kierie with his own two hands. Let him come and see for himself what his useless bastard has destroyed this time.

No U-Turn

I was about to put the art magazine back into the oven because it's the best hiding place in the house, but the squealing tyres and the approaching siren distracted me, so I forgot what I'd been doing, and left the magazine on the chair by the TV.

The oven hasn't worked since we moved to this house overlooking the freeway near the airport. When my father is hungry, I heat cans of beans on the stovetop or make scrambled eggs. Usually the sirens come and go along the freeway, but this one screeches to a halt next door. Blue lights flicker on the walls and ceiling. I watch what's happening at the neighbour's from the window while Pa sleeps.

I hide my paints and brushes in the oven, too. The magazine series was advertised on TV, right after the programme on landscapes. A lady with brown pigtails smiled reassuringly from her portable easel in a green meadow beside a blue lake. She whisked the paint over a dampened page, transforming the empty space into a masterpiece in minutes. I couldn't believe it was so easy. Then the lady promised a starter pack with new colours every week, and professional tips on creating your own work of art.

Three more police vans arrive, sirens blaring. The dog howls.

The painter on TV had said that once you start, your soul opens up and there's no going back. Your creativity blossoms and life is beautiful. I slide my finished paintings into old newspapers, burying them at the bottom of the stack while he sleeps. Often they don't dry quickly enough and newsprint seeps in, spoiling them.

Policemen run to the back of the Chinaman's house.

I'd like to sit in a green meadow by a blue lake. The only landscape from here is the grey view of the highway with warehouses and factories beyond.

Officers stand behind trees, kneel behind walls, guns pointing at the house; another bangs on the door, then crouches beside the doorframe. The sirens keep blaring, but still Pa sleeps.

Last month I hid my magazine under the dog's blanket at the bottom of her basket – the issue with sketching tips. The old dog didn't like my magazine there. After we'd gone to bed, she scratched it out. In the morning, the charcoal sketches of a naked girl were strewn across the floor. I'd woken early to let the dog out. Luckily I found the torn pieces before my father woke. I stuck them together with sticky tape.

More police cars arrive. More policemen run around the house, squatting behind their vehicles, pointing guns. The dog sits on my feet, shaking. At the first shot, she piddles on the floor. My father wakes, bellowing from the next room, Stop the goddamned noise. Then two policemen break down the door to the neighbour's house. More shots and my father storms into the kitchen, sleep in his eyes, yelling, What the fuck?

A policeman got shot, I say, pointing at a staggering man who crumples on the steps. The dog wags her tail and limps over to my father, who has moved to the window.

The country has gone to the dogs, says my father.

Another policeman is dragging his buddy towards the ambulance that's just arrived. Bring me a drink, says my father, heading for the chair in front of the TV. I can't bear this shit another minute.

It's too late to hide that art magazine now.

Yield

I was about to put the cinnamon buns in the oven that I'd turned on low, when a crow flew against the kitchen window. I'd been peering into the open door, adjusting the racks to make space for the buns to rise without sticking against the upper rack. My hands were safe and deep in the big oven gloves, a wedding present from my mother-in-law.

She has taken me under her wing. She says she always wanted another boy-chick to love. My mother refused to attend the ceremony, calling the San Francisco rabbi who married us an ungodly liberal. She attended the reception grudgingly, but hated the sushi.

I looked up, startled by the bang, and saw the bird bouncing off. It left a shadowy imprint of feathers against the glass. The day was tainted. I knew there'd be bad news.

The coffee I'd brewed no longer smelled sweet. There'd be mishaps and stubbed toes, fights and dropped vases. Maybe a catastrophe.

I showered while the buns warmed through, fearful that the phone would ring, announcing death, fearful that I'd slip in a puddle and break my wrist, ending up in hospital.

After drying and dressing, I took the cinnamon buns out of the oven, anticipating another bump on the window, another suicidal crow, a spook. With shaking hands, I took the tray through to my love, who was working on his latest composition, a symphony commissioned by the Ministry of Arts and Culture. They needed a musical reflection on the ten years since the Truth and Reconciliation Commission laid bare the nation's soul.

When he plays "Past Your Eyes, Your Past" on the piano, it sounds like the hounds of hell baying for blood. The National Orchestra will play it at the Grahamstown Festival. The first time I heard it pronounced, I heard, "Pasteurise your past." He laughed, saying maybe that's what we've done.

He set aside the bassoon part, fitting the lid back on his fountain pen. As I settled the tray on his knees, he fondled my balls. What's up, my dove, he asked, what's on your heart? I snuggled under the duvet beside him. It's going to be a hideous day, I said. A crow flew into the window. It's an omen. I bet the doctor calls to tell me my CD count has fallen.

He tousled my hair. Stay in bed. The whole day? I asked. Go on, he said. How decadent is that? I asked. Force yourself, he said.

Stop

I was about to put my head in the oven, to wipe out the sooty crumbs of all the casseroles and roasts and puddings that boil and spill, when my knees started to complain.

My knees said, Mama, you are too old for this. My head said, hush knees. But my knees are too cheeky. They wouldn't let up.

I couldn't reach the corners easily and I didn't want to press on the oven door, because if I broke it, the baas would dock my pay. That happened last month, when I dropped a teacup that cost too too much to replace. Oh Jesu, it still hurts to think of that beautiful cup in pieces on this very kitchen floor.

So I moved sideways to reach in, but kneeling and twisting at a funny angle, my back started to grumble.

My back said, Mama, you've been a domestic worker for fifty years. It's enough. My head said, be quiet, back. There's another grandchild filling my daughter's belly. My son's got no work. Somebody has to buy the school shoes this month if there are no more breakages.

I was scrubbing the oven window from the inside with a tired pot scourer and a lot of elbow grease. Not steel wool that scratches the glass. Not the strong spray that makes the glass sparkle in minutes. My madam doesn't buy cleaning fluids with poisonous chemicals any more. Toxic, she says.

My fingers and my elbow and my shoulder became angry. They shouted at me: Mama, you are sixty-five. We are in agreement: you are too old for this kneeling on the white people's floor.

Eish, I said. I am afraid.

My body said, phone that clever lawyer that helped your friend to sue her employer for docking her wages because she broke the vacuum cleaner. Phone that woman now. You are not a girl any more.

Snap

YOUR HAIR IS BEAUTIFUL, Ouma, like jacaranda blossoms. Did Mom colour it for you? Here, your mirror. Can you see? Is the angle right? Mom says you can't speak, but sometimes you sing. How does that work? Never mind. I know how hard answering questions is when you can't talk. My tongue has become shy. In the group sessions at Tara, the hospital where I've been admitted, they call that resistance; they call it passive aggression.

I've brought some photos I took on outings for good behaviour. Took them with my new camera, the one I bought with the money you gave me for my birthday. It's bigger and heavier than the old one, has a great chunky lens. At first I could hardly hold it steady. I must have clicked a hundred times. Maybe five hundred. That's possible with a digital camera. Delete the blurred images, the tilted horizons, the overexposed subject from a light too bright.

I picked out the best ones. Mom said to bring no more than ten. She said not to overwhelm you. I could put them on your wall. Here, beside your bed. I have a picture of Barrister next to my bed. I miss him. A lot. Especially his thumping tail that whacks against my legs when he's pleased. Do you miss Pixie? I should smuggle her in here, tell the nurse she's your pet therapist. Mom says you're like a child now. Is that right? And if it is, how old are you? Two? Or four? A little older?

This first one is of the dilapidated jetty at Zoo Lake. We went there on the first outing after my admission. I'd earned my place on the old beige bus by gaining 200 grams. If your weight goes up, you get treats and privileges, like being allowed to wash your hair or take a walk. If your weight goes down, hard luck, you lose the right to go to the toilet unsupervised. I don't think about that too much, but I do think about my work. There are photos to make of the lost and found, of containers and holding places. I'm preparing a portfolio for my next exhibition. I prefer the viewfinder even though the digital camera has a viewing window that displays a bigger version of what you're looking at. It's simpler looking at the world in a limited way.

This next picture is a close-up of the hull of a rowboat. I wanted to capture the texture of the algae against the shiny yellow paint and the inky black water. The colours, so vibrant against the dull trees and dark water. It works, don't you think? You'd have loved boating. We rowed out on a brilliant green boat, right up to the fountain in the middle of the lake. I went with Safiya and Sherezade. They're twins and patients in the unit. Joined at the hip, says the nurse. They took turns at pulling the oars while I took pictures.

They told me how every weekend they go there with their whole family, a tribe of nieces and nephews and aunties and uncles, and their grandmother, tottering in heels. What a matriarch she is, telling everybody where to go, what to bring, where to set the picnic and light fires, when to start cooking, chasing the children off to the swings, and so on. No disrespect, Ouma, but you were never a matriarch. You were scared of my mother too, weren't you? Still are, I guess. Hey! Did you wiggle your finger? You agree? Oh, Ouma, that tells me I'm right.

Once we'd docked again Safiya and Sherezade stood side by side on the rocks at the water's edge. Thuli, the

African model, who reminds us daily that top fashion photographers are killing themselves to shoot her, pointed out the bridge where the Face of Africa was filmed last year. She was a finalist, she says. She's the next big thing, she says. The next Alek Wek, the next Tyra Banks, the next Liya Kebede. She claims it was dehydration that got her rushed to hospital and eliminated, but it wasn't that. I know her secret. What can I say? Photographers see everything.

The rocks, would you believe it, are not genuine. A high-traffic spot on the path had weakened, catching Thuli's stiletto. Beneath the fibreglass shell, frayed netting showed through, like string packing-bags for oranges and gem squash, filled with concrete. While Thuli clucked at her scratched heel, I took a photo of the interior of the fake rock. I used the macro settings. I didn't bring it, though. It isn't pretty.

This one is, though. Safiya and Sherezade held hands as they looked down into the water, so still, that it offered back a perfect reflection. I shot the photo from the bridge, angling it to frame the quartet. Did Safiya see herself or her sister when she looked in the water? Who does Sherezade see when she looks in a mirror? You can hardly tell them apart. Identical. Up close, there's a scar on Safiya's cheek, shaped like a tiny, cupped palm. If you know where to look.

It was my first outing since my admission. A reward for good behaviour, but I felt wobbly, like my legs couldn't stand up to people's stares. The waitresses at the outdoor café whispered behind their hands. We walked three times round the lake before stopping to buy sugar-free gum. Sherezade said we shouldn't overdo the exercise. We couldn't lose weight on an outing. That wouldn't do at all. They'd already exerted themselves on the water.

You can't see, Ouma? Shall I help you with your specs? Talking about outings, this isn't exactly an outing. It's something like goodbye. Mom says you've only got days, maybe hours. They let me out for that.

The peculiar thing about Safiya and Sherezade is their rhythm: they wake up and fall asleep at exactly the same moment. They bathe and dress simultaneously, their clothes and hairstyles are identical. They even stir and sip their tea in unison. We ordered herbal tea. Safiya said it's sophisticated. Slimming too, she said, while fingering sugar sachets with spidery fingers.

Were you there when I was born, Ouma? Did you see my twin sister? I wish you could tell me more about our birth.

Later we watched the ducks checking us out, trying to decide whether we were good for any scraps of bread. You could tell they were hungry. They did that thing where they just stood and swayed, staring, looking about to faint. The slow walk I recognised. It's how I move when it's too much effort to lift my foot another time. The ducks seemed reluctant to swim, too tired to get in the water.

But when a young mother arrived at a table next to us, setting the brake on a stroller before lifting her baby out, they perked up. The baby toddled towards them, grasping a heel of bread in his chubby fist. The ducks, which were as tall as he was, pecked the bread rudely, nipping his hand. He screamed until his mother hitched him onto her hip and kissed his knuckles. The ducks, all hissing and swaying necks, clamoured about with their creepy impenetrable stares until a waiter shooed them off with a tray.

The baby eased off his sobbing as his mother spooned applesauce from a round glass jar into his open mouth. He waved and kicked, greeting each spoonful eagerly. Distracted by the applesauce escaping onto his bib, his mother didn't notice the bee hovering over her cheesecake, then landing in her mango juice. Mid-way through the next spoonful, while waiting for him to open his mouth, she leaned over her drink and sipped on her straw. I raised my arm in a warning gesture, tried to say, no, stop. But before I could speak, she'd sucked the bee up the straw. She jerked in horror, hands flying to her mouth as it stung her tongue. The spoon catapulted over the stroller and the jar of baby food bounced off the table into the dirt. The woman squealed, Ow, ow, ow! Her baby banged his fists, enraged at this new insult. I dashed over to comfort the baby, trying to hold him. But he was too heavy and slipped from my embrace, screaming louder.

His mother flapped me away as though I were another pesky duck. I backed away to our table, ashamed at my incompetence, unable to hold back my tears. Safiya felt sorry for me, but she misread my grief. She said I probably hadn't done permanent damage to my reproductive system. Sherezade patted my arm, saying, You can still have a baby... But it wasn't that. I don't want a baby of my own. I'd failed to hold that child in his distress.

This photo shows the occupational therapy projects, the pencil boxes and octagonal jewellery holders in various stages of decoupage. After painting our boxes, we glued on pictures cut from magazines or wrapping paper, followed by layers of varnish. Thuli whined about the mindlessness of it all. Expanded nursery-school programme, she grumbled. Then she sang off-key: *Idle hands are the devil's playthings, the devil's playthings, the devil's playthings...* It beats fidgeting around a Monopoly board for hours with odd cards and houses missing from the box. Safiya and Sherezade painted matching purple jewellery boxes.

Safiya paged through a *Living & Loving*, ripping out pictures of babies to stick on her box so that her mother could use it for storing ear buds or nappy clips. Sherezade wanted none of it. She found a large sheet of giftwrap decorated with dragonflies, and pushed it over to her sister. Then she spun the scissors across the tabletop.

The decoupage must dry properly between stages. Then one rubs it with fine sandpaper till it's smooth and even. It's the perfect leisure activity for the obsessive-compulsives of the world. Thuli uses her hairdryer to perfect her finish. She uses it on her nails too, when she paints them the colour of burnt toast. The other shade she likes is coffee grits. I rushed my project, and now it's wrinkled.

This photo is of Safiya and Sherezade's feet, Ouma. Look here, even the curl of their toes at the pointy part of their shoes is the same. Both wear down on the inside of the heel first with their matching long-legged gait. How do you suppose it works – that twin thing? If I could watch my twin do all the things I do, I would know what made me *me*. If Marly's right sneaker also wore out at the toe first, surely I'd know what's bothering this body? I'd be able to see myself.

You want some water? Here. Need another sip?

For example, I'd know why I can't control my pinky when I sew. It spikes out doing this jerky clown dance when I'm stitching. We were embroidering bookmarks for Mother's Day. Safiya and Sherezade were creating identical funky chain-stitch patterns in white on matching strips of turquoise cloth. They don't say anything to each other. They seldom talk anyway. They simply started stitching without looking at each other's work. Their needles pricked through, forming the loop and pulling the tail in smooth gestures, no tugging or fuss. Like musical instruments playing a melody at the same tempo, in the same key.

I couldn't concentrate on my own bookmark. The nurse

came along and said, "I know you've got issues with your mother, but you still have to complete this project. You don't have to give it to her, you know. Keep it for yourself on Mother's Day. You're becoming a mother to yourself now, aren't you? Make something pretty for you." So I started, but there was nobody to pace myself with, no exterior rhythm, no internal drive, while Safiya and Sherezade cut new threads and knotted them simultaneously.

While they rethreaded their needles, Safiya looked up and noticed my little finger waggling in and out.

I giggled with them. Their laughter wasn't unkind. But an hour later, Safiya and Sherezade had the same eccentric daisies swaying across their bookmark, and I was tumbling across an abandoned field, light as a dandelion. I wanted to talk to that other me, my mirror that should be out in the world. I wanted to ask her why she does all the sick things she does. I'd say to Marly: Why are you here, in the hospital? Why won't you eat?

You see, Ouma, I know I'm not fat. They say anorexics have a distorted body image. Not me. I know I'm emaciated. My nose and jaw and forehead are too big for my face. The art therapist had us lie on huge sheets of paper and drew a line around our bodies. Then we had to fill in all the beauty inside us, separating it from the hurt outside. We were told to clothe our stick-like limbs in beautiful intentions. I've read the textbooks. I go to therapy. I have shame issues, control issues, boundary issues and repressed sexuality issues. Could the list be more boring? But it isn't the truth. Despite my sub-optimal cognition, I really *do* know that what I'm doing is stupid. I *get* that I'm starving my brain cells, closing the door on future options.

Oh, goodness, you need a tissue. Here, I've got one for you.

What does Safiya say to Sherezade when they're alone?

They never talk to each other when people are around. They don't even talk through other people, like Mom and Dad do. I sneak into the bathroom when I know they're in adjacent bathing cubicles. They never talk over the divider like other patients. They just swing their matching towels, the colour of bruised aubergines, over the top of the adjacent doors as if in one movement, then switch the taps on, then off, at precisely the same moment, as if marking the steps of some bizarre ballet. Then they emerge, wearing the same outfit, the same jasmine scent.

At visiting hour, their mother bustles in, surly and hairy, trailing their six younger brothers and sisters, a toddler at her knee, an infant on her hip, and a new bump in front. The middle ones in their gymslips and polished school shoes, the older ones wearing headscarves and jeans. She frets because her eldest girls are supposed to write matric this year. She frets because they are bringing shame on the family. The prospective in-laws want to know that there will be a string of little brown babies, and the girls haven't had their periods in over a year. They're enrolled at a prestigious private college and share the class medals equally between them. She frets about that, too. Clever girls are no great blessing as far as their mother is concerned. Or at least that's what Safiya says in group therapy.

In private, Safiya told me about the pact they made to stave off the orchestrated double wedding. They were betrothed to suitable boys on their tenth birthday, but they both want to go to university to study microbiology. Makes sense, doesn't it? It has a beautiful, if painful, logic. They're on a hunger strike to claim their intellectual, social and sexual freedom. How clever do the doctors have to be to figure that out?

Ouma, are you comfortable? Can I plump your pillows?

I hope the doctors looking after you are smarter than the ones looking after us.

When the nutritionist said – did you notice they are called nutritionists, and not dieticians? Too many negative connotations to the word "diet". "Nutrition" is a word with nurturing rather than punitive associations. Ha! Anyway, the nutritionist was saying that even after treatment, normal menstruation never returns in twenty-five per cent of cases of severe anorexia. The twins smirked. As if that was their ultimate goal – to put on just enough weight to get out of hospital so that they can return as fast as they can to starving themselves under the protection of their burkas.

As I was saying, Ouma, in this photo, I've focused on the straps of their shoes, which peel over at exactly the same spot. I wish I could look at my sister's shoes. Apparently I ate her before I was born. That's what my mother told me. She said I came out fat and round and red from swallowing all her blood. Marly was tiny and thin, pale and eternally perfect. We went to her grave again last weekend. We go on the first Sunday of every month. We left fresh lilies with their buds still tightly closed in the vase cemented to her headstone.

My parents always fought on the first Sunday of each month. For as many years as I can remember, my mother would call my father an insensitive brute, and he would beg her to stop resurrecting the dead. After we celebrated our twenty-first birthday last year, my father refused to go ever again. The party's over, he said.

I stood beside Mom while she adjusted the lilies and sobbed into her handkerchief. Then she asked for private time. I wandered through the other graves. The ones that always intrigue me are the "double bed" arrangements, where a name and date are engraved on one side, and the other side is empty, waiting for the partner left behind. It's pragmatic. There's no space for me beside Marly. Besides, even if there was, it's much too late for me to be buried in the infant section now.

This photo is from the ward kitchen, Ouma. The camera felt solid in my hand that day. My arm felt stable, stronger, maybe. Notice how the light from the window catches the dents in the pot? The steam curls out, the dents in the side, the sliver of onion caught on the edge. We made vegetable soup to sell to the patients in the other wards. It was a fundraiser. We are supposed to contribute to the expenses of the outings, and Safiya suggested the idea. Then there was a quarrel about what kind of soup to make. Thuli suggested pea and ham. Safiya and Sherezade wrinkled their noses at exactly the same moment, and Safiya said the Jewish and Muslim patients couldn't eat pig. Thuli said in her fake American accent that educated people say "pork" not "pig". Another girl said we should make chicken soup for the soul. But then someone else said it wasn't vegetarian. So they agreed on minestrone. It's hard to photograph minestrone when it's hot. The steam condenses on the lens. Food photography is pure bamboozlement and hoodwinks, Ouma. You cannot imagine the dirty tricks of kitchen studios, the glycerin, toothpicks, white glue and paintbrushes.

Are you warm enough? Want a shawl around your shoulders?

Thuli had commandeered the pot, one thin dark hand stirring, the other grasping the pale wooden handle of the pot, which appeared fat in her grip. I'd adjusted the setting to cancel the flash, thinking of the natural light, but when she heard the shutter click she threw the ladle at me, screeching, calling me a fucking wannabe snoop. She's wrong on all counts. I'm no wannabe. I'm published,

Ouma. My by-line is everywhere, *Getaway*, *Weg*, *Africa Geographic*. I have exhibited. Just because I'm not a fashion photographer doesn't mean shit. But why do I even bother?

If the nurses knew that Thuli was sniffing cocaine under their nose, they'd call the cops and have her arrested. But she's sly. She waits till everyone's asleep. Her bed is in the corner, opposite mine. She sneaks off to the loo after lights out, once the night nurse is dozing. On her return, she leans over my bed to check that I'm asleep. I keep my breathing slow and deep. She prods me, calls my name. I fake a loose-jawed snore. Then she reaches into her cupboard, brings out a sandal she never wears and unscrews the heel. She removes a tiny baggie and forms a line on the top of her bedside table. She uncaps a cheap Bic, removing the nib and back end before snorting. I'm the only one who knows what she's up to. I told you, Ouma, photographers see everything.

While we made soup, I watched Safiya peeling potatoes with military precision, each peel exactly one inch long. I saw Sherezade pick up a fleck of grated carrot and put it in her mouth. She chewed it twenty times, then spat it into a tissue and threw it in the bin.

Anyway, after the ladle-throwing scene, Thuli got some or other punishment, but my camera was taken away for three days. It felt like my hands were chopped off, my arms so empty I couldn't sew, couldn't take notes in the nutrition lectures, couldn't even brush my hair. I could hardly bear to pick up my food, but if I lost a gram, I'd never get my camera back. I could have ratted on Thuli, but it was too much hassle. It's not that I don't want to talk; it's more like I can't. The psychologist tries in our twice-weekly sessions. Her top lip quivers when I finally respond to her questions. Then it tightens again in forced empathy, and my bones contract with the wrong answer.

It's as if the dead baby I consumed is still inside me, eating all my words and spitting out the rejects. My language limps off my tongue when I try to speak. I don't mean what I say; I can't say what I mean. It's all jumbled. The nutritionist warned us about this. She said brain scans indicate that parts of the brain undergo structural changes and abnormal activity during anorexic states. Some people return to normal after weight gain, but others never recover fully. She flipped her chart and wrote in spiky red letters: Studies show that brain damage may be PERMANENT.

I can't help wondering: if our birth had been different, if Marly were alive today, would her feet hit the ground like mine? Would she also listen to Leonard Cohen, knowing how the end of the world sounds like a famous blue raincoat? Would she also wear only cotton and refuse polyester or nylon? Would she detest liquorice and aniseed? Would she hold a camera balanced in the pad of her thumb, legs crossed and braced for stability? Would her hip and elbow jut out for balance?

And this photo, Ouma, is of the fishpond filled now with dry and papery leaves. A patient from Ward Eight drowned. He went out for a cigarette after dark and ambled down a path on a moonless night. Maybe he stumbled on the uneven ground and fell into the water, too dazed to save himself. He'd had shock therapy that day; he was confused. Maybe they fried his survival instinct by accident. Maybe it was suicide. How do you drown in knee-deep water, Ouma? Can it be so easy? If you had the choice, would you leave?

When I saw two policemen in a van talking to the guards at the entrance as I jogged around the grounds early that morning, my first thought was, Yesss! They've come for Thuli; the vain bitch is going to jail. Horrible, aren't I? But the van didn't stop outside our unit. It rattled on down the road, heaving over the bumps, to the wards at the bottom of the hill. I followed it down the road and waited behind a big pin oak, catching my breath, while the ward manager described his grim find. The officers radioed for the mortuary van before setting off on foot. I ran on, passing the old fountain where a posse of doctors stood in the cold, stamping their feet. His jacket, like a skin, floated on the surface. I almost wished I'd had the idea first. They've drained the pond now, not wanting copycats.

There's a schoolgirl who filmed her suicide, Ouma. She blogged about it. Told the world what she was going to do. Now that is macabre. Her mother was watching *The Bold and the Beautiful* in the next room. Her father had gone to the station to buy smokes. He found her on his return, hanging from the dog's leash strung up from the ceiling. She'd set up the video on a tripod.

I have photos that I can't show and didn't bring. I used the timer to create self-portraits. You've never judged or condemned, never ordered me to eat. You never said I was making Mom suffer. You never called me manipulative. Your heart ached, though, I know. But those photos, the ones I probably shouldn't talk about, I take them, Ouma, to search myself. I want to see what's under my skin. Is she there? I open myself up looking for her. But there's nothing, not even a lock of her hair. All I find is soft netting, wet concrete.

I look at those pictures and pretend that I'm Marly. I imagine her now: fat, red and devouring, staring back at her anemic other. As I look at those pictures I'm transfused, falling through a mirror.

You can't take the photos over, Ouma, but can you take Marly a jacaranda bloom? Play with her, like you did with me. Make her laugh, Ouma. And then say it's enough. Ask her to let it go. Tell her to stop.

Boston
Brown Bread

RENIER AHRENDS jerked his son's homework assignment off the fridge door. The fairy magnet that had held it in place popped off and broke as it hit the floor. Renier kicked the snapped-off ballet slipper under the fridge and smacked the magnet back in place.

"Is *this* supposed to represent advancement in education?" he asked, thrusting the paper in his wife's face. His voice, which had once been a pure baritone, was now a rasping growl. She bit her lip and kept paging through the recipe book.

The crest of the Welkom Preparatory School at the top of the page contained a stylised swallow that swooped above a squiggled scroll bearing the school's motto, like the one on Peet's new blazer. He'd been there just one term.

When a young black man had been promoted ahead of Renier at the Johannesburg head office, Renier manoeuvered a transfer to the mining town where traditional values still thrived. Just three years off retirement, he believed he might yet avoid the humiliation of answering to a black "baas" who was also, he said, an inexperienced fool, an incompetent ass. His wife had wondered privately whether his attitude – and not simply his chain-smoking – had given him throat cancer. She'd said, more diplomatically, that he shouldn't speak so harshly. He swore at that, saying he'd give up cigarettes before he kissed a kaffir's arse.

Renier flicked the homework assignment, pronouncing the school motto with punctilious clarity, "Sa-pi-en-ti-a et Ve-ri-tas." He scowled as his son adjusted the oven temperature. "I bet not one kid in your class even knows what language this is, let alone its meaning."

Peet knew what it meant. He also knew it was unwise to reveal his knowledge with his father in this mood. Pa would either repeat the ghastly tale of how he had been taught Greek *and* Latin by masters who reinforced lessons with heavy rulers on dull boys' knuckles, or he would demand the notice announcing the season's rugby fixtures.

Peet hadn't tried out for the rugby team, and he hadn't told Pa either. The grunting and heaving of so many bodies made him nervous. He felt claustrophobic in the scrum. He preferred the company of gentle Mr Bouwer, who taught him to play the recorder and conducted the senior primary choir. When the music teacher sent home notices of rehearsals and concerts, Peet lost them at the bottom of his satchel.

"Isn't that right, son? Do you know what the motto means?" asked his father.

Peet nodded. He would wait until Pa had had a brandy or two before he risked saying anything. His father's mood improved when his mother poured him a drink, but she was busy. Her hands were sticky, stirring the sludgy mixture in the bowl.

Peet wondered whether he should offer to pour one. But if his father were to say, as he did last time, "So Mummy's little helper thinks Daddy needs a little helper, does he?" then his mother would start crying, and nobody would speak to anybody for the rest of the day. At this stage of the weekend, his parents were still talking. Things usually went downhill after lunch on Saturday, although today it looked like it was starting early.

Renier read the instructions for the latest school project:

All Grade Seven learners will participate in Global Culture Month as part of the Life Orientation programme.

In Week One, learners must research the dominant lifestyle of the country they have been assigned.

He gave his son a dark look. "Life Orientation, or *Lifestyle* Orientation?"

Your child is requested to bring a typical food item from this country. Learners must prepare a five-minute speech on their topic. Your child has been assigned…

"America" was written in Miss Smit's graceful script. Peet knew it wasn't really a country, that the Americas were two continents. His mother levelled a cup of rye flour with the back of a knife. She'd bought the flour at the only health-food store in town. She passed it to Peet, showing no sign of having heard her husband.

"I ask you with tears in my eyes, haven't we heard enough from America to last a hundred lifetimes?"

In Week Two, learners should bring music from the country they are studying. They will be taught how to download sound clips from the internet in their Design & Technology class.

"And what's this about downloading sound clips from the internet? Let's breed a nation of copyright pirates! Is that the way to go?"

Peet shrugged. His mother said, "I have no idea."

"Those 'educators' I'm paying so bloody much haven't got a freaking clue. Don't even think of downloading anything at home unless you plan to go to jail. For a long time. That's plain and simple copyright violation."

In Week Three, learners research the habits of the indigenous peoples of the region using periodicals like 'National Geographic'.

"Indigenous people? Oh puh-lease. Who's studying South Africa? You're going to come home having learned to say, 'Eish!' and 'Heita!' and 'Yebo-yes!'"

Peet would never speak slang like that at home. He couldn't even get it right at school. Black boys didn't want to play with him unless he took marbles to the playground, and then they beat him at the game. When he aimed at the target, his shot bounced wildly over the sandy terrain. He'd stopped buying marbles because other boys always went home with their pockets bulging with his.

At break, he'd taken to slipping into the music block to practise his recorder instead. Mr Bouwer had entered him for a Trinity College exam, and there were lots of scales to memorise. He never practised at home unless his father was away.

In Week Four, learners focus on Language and Literature (details to follow).

"Did you hear me?" Renier demanded.

"Uh huh," said his wife.

Peet said nothing.

"And now Britney Spears is on the new curriculum, and you're studying the poetry of 'Overprotected'?"

Peet tipped the flour into the sieve with the baking soda and salt. He wondered what Mr Bouwer thought of Britney Spears. They'd never discussed her. Mr Bouwer played CDs of the Amsterdam Loeki Quartet. He'd let slip that he once had a lover who played in that ensemble. Peet had looked at the CD cover, but he couldn't see any women in the group. The picture of the players was very small though, and he couldn't be certain.

Peet flushed just thinking about Mr Bouwer, and spilled flour on the counter. His mother said nothing. If his father hadn't been there, she might have said, "Careful now, darling," or, "Wipe that up, my love," but she held the sieve with hands that were starting to shake. Peet took it from her and turned the spindle. He watched the dry ingredients form a pointy mine dump in the bowl below.

"Way-way-wait. Let me guess. We ditch a Eurocentric system to fawn over American imperialists and our son must study it? This is what Outcomes-Based Education is all about?"

"Perhaps," said his mother.

"And this is *acceptable* to you?"

The boy stirred the bowl with a cracked wooden spoon. He wondered why his mother kept it. She always said that germs collected in cracks. But she also said that germs were killed by heat. There were lots of other countries on Miss Smit's list: hot countries like Bolivia and Chile, cold countries like Denmark, Great Britain, France. It was a pity his surname was Ahrends. Miss Smit had assigned the countries alphabetically.

Peet poured a slow stream of Lyle's Molasses-Flavoured Golden Syrup into the buttermilk, which had pooled in the bottom of the mixer. Pure molasses was unavailable in Welkom, his mother had said. She thought one might be able to get it at Thrupps in Johannesburg.

The ingredients swirled into a uniform toffee-coloured mixture. Peet wondered if it would have upset his father less if he'd come home to find them cooking Bolivian bean broth.

"Can't he just take a Big Mac to school?" asked Renier.

"No," said his mother, closing the flour bag with a clothes peg. At the library, they had found the Betty Crocker Cookery Book. His mother said she wished they still lived in Johannesburg. Peet wished he lived in Boston.

The recipe required Graham flour. Peet had looked that up in the Oxford dictionary. "Graham" was an adjective of North American origin, denoting unsifted whole-wheat flour, or biscuits or bread made from this, e.g., Graham Crackers.

"He could take Barbie Pre-mix Cookies," suggested his father.

"He could not," replied his mother.

She had told him as they stood in the dry goods aisle that Snowflake's Nutty Wheat was similar to Graham flour, and cornmeal was like mealie meal. His mother had been to America. He very much hoped she was right.

Peet read some stuff on the internet about Reverend Sylvester Graham:

A Presbyterian minister, Sylvester Graham was born in 1794. He believed that physical lust and masturbation were harmful to the body, causing dire maladies like pulmonary consumption, spinal diseases, epilepsy, and insanity, as well as lesser afflictions like headaches and indigestion. Too much lust could cause the early death of offspring, who would have been conceived from weakened stock. He died in 1851.

Peet wondered whether Boston Brown Bread would remedy his frequent urge to stroke himself. Perhaps it would also cure the feeling that arose when Mr Bouwer sat beside him at the music stand. Sometimes he slouched deliberately, so that Mr Bouwer would place his hand at the base of his spine, reminding him to sit straight.

"Is our son learning about imperial conversion or the history of North America?" asked Renier, staring at the recipe in pounds and ounces.

"Looks like it," said his mother, handing Peet a damp cloth. First he brushed the excess flour that had fallen on the counter into his hand. Then he shook it into the bin, and wiped the counter.

"Looks like what?" asked Renier.

The boy took a few raisins from the cup and slipped them into his pocket.

"Probably both," said his mother.

She opened the fridge and removed the folded butter wrappers stored under the freezer compartment. Peet greased the inside of the transparent pudding bowl. He held it up to the light to inspect a line running from the chipped edge to its centre. The butter formed a ridge along the line. He ran his finger along it, trying to smooth it out. If his father had not been there, he would have shown his mother the unusual feature.

"So is the Minister of Education trying to produce a new breed of global traders, a nation of international merchants – or what?" asked his father.

"Dunno," said his mother, spooning the batter into the bowl.

Peet scraped the bowl clean with the floppy spatula. He licked his fingers. They tasted of cinnamon.

"We're educating our son to be a 'new age man'?" asked his father, forming quotation marks in the air.

Peet wiped his greasy hands on a paper towel before rinsing them under the hot tap, and then fixed the lid in place.

"Maybe," said his mother re-boiling the kettle. Peet held a length of tape, which she cut in longish pieces.

"Or is this 'Restoration of Family Values 101'?"

His mother taped down the lid with firm strokes of her thumb and placed it in the roasting pan ready for steaming. "I suppose it is," she said.

"I'm paying private school fees for my son to bake American cakes at home?"

His mother poured boiling water into the roasting pan. As it touched the glassware, a sharp crack split the silence. The bowl fractured in a clear arc. The man and the boy stared at the pudding that oozed slowly through the gaping slit.

"Ja," said Peet's mother, staring directly at her husband, "I guess you are."

Peet felt for the raisins in his pocket. They were soft and squishy on his finger tips. "Get another bowl," said his mother, "our job's not finished yet."

The boy opened the cupboard where the bowls were stacked in a tilted pile. His hands were still greasy. His mother wanted a bowl perched mid-way down the stack. He took a raisin from his pocket and secreted it in one ear. He pushed it in further, twisting his pinky, then did the same with the other ear. He could fit another raisin in. And another, and another.

Nymph

THE WAITER AT MEZZALUNA SHOWS you to a seat at a yellowwood table on the uneven stoep. Across the road is a boutique with burglar bars on the windows, wrought-iron curlicues with semi-circular rays expanding toward the glass edges. In the middle, the metal curves form a sunrise. An old man on a red bench sits in front of the window, obscuring the solar centre of the bars. Where the fiery core should be, he is scratching his stomach.

You're trying to work out why you still tell Jonah he's your blessing, a thing you do out of habit, or duty. His dithering is no longer endearing: the hesitation at green lights, the backwards and forwards between pot and plate, the way he slows in the passage, preparing an apology for an imagined infraction, some wrong he hasn't done. Once he said, "I do," but now it's always, "I'm sorry. I'm sorry. I'm sorry."

You used to listen to everything he said, when you still hoped there was a chance that a brain scan would explain things, and that pills could fix the problem. You'd try to reassure him, but you can no longer endure his half-sentences, the invisible torment. When he speaks in a low stutter, you don't try to fill in the gaps any more. There was a time you thought he'd get better, but now you snap at him: "Jonah! Why are you sorry? What have you done?" You can't forgive a non-slight. The texture of the beaten metal of the burglar bars takes you back to the blacksmith you interviewed in Hartbeesfontein, back when you worked for a trade magazine. You've forgotten his name,

133

but you remember the heat the day your shutter clicked to capture the smooth welding he did at his furnace. Such deserted roads you drove to find his smallholding. So far away, you could have been in Australia. All bluegums and dust. No passing cars. Just his dogs. And a helper whose name you didn't catch.

Once you were gentle with Jonah, hoping you could help him if you stayed calm and talked nicely. You'd say, "Ease up, Bean, your brain is just playing tricks." But you've stopped bothering to soothe. You no longer say "It's okay" and "Don't worry." You don't withhold your own affectionate caresses because your body has its own compulsions, and your hand seeks out his skin with the inevitability of a compass spinning north. You wish your strokes were reciprocated, but they aren't, and you fear that soon you will slip into tenderness with another.

A puppy with a quivering snout slept under the blacksmith's workbench, unperturbed by the ringing hammers, the hiss of the white-hot metal thrust into cold water. Its huge paws twitched as the bellows of the smith pitched and gasped.

You wanted it all that different day: the humble cottage, the dogs, the wind in the papery leaves that soughed in the heat. You ached for the blacksmith's body, even though he was a stranger. Because he was. You watched the moon, full and lonely, wishing you could reach up and pluck it out of the afternoon sky. You took no photo because your camera would have reduced the moon to a sorry speck, devoid of magic. When it was time to go, you shook hands with the blacksmith, clutching your private desire.

Later you stared at the photos of his hands, wishing you'd felt the copper bracelet around his wrist. You had photographed the tattoo that ran like a hoof track down the back of his legs, disappearing into the leather sandals that contained his big feet, solid on the earth. Behind his goggles he hadn't noticed where you aimed your lens.

That night you'd said to Jonah, "Come, Bean, come to bed." But the sweetness was gone from your voice. You bristled as Jonah slurped his water and gulped his pills. You flinched when he put the glass down on the wood, tethered your mouth while a watermark pooled on the bedside table. If you'd pointed it out, he'd have rubbed at it a hundred times, saying, "I'm sorry. I'm sorry. I'm sorry." When he retreated to the bathroom you replaced the glass on the coaster and dried the wood with a tissue.

There's a dress behind the bars of the boutique, a wedding dress, oyster voile with an ivory satin sash, low on the waist. Amber beads circle the neck of the headless dummy, armless and unarmed in the boutique window. In front of the bridal gown in the window, a slow motion catches your eye. The man waves a paper back and forth, then holds it up to his eyes. He reads slowly, mouthing the words.

It's your favourite place, this restaurant with the gold wooden window frames surrounded by wisteria leaves, fresh and green. A through-breeze cools the morning, and the fronds of the winding vines yield, fluttering in the sunlight. It's one place you'll never show Jonah. Its antique gramophones, bay windows and red concrete floor are yours alone. Under the high, pressed ceilings flits a secret you can't share because he will spoil it with apologies.

Last night you suppressed a sigh even as the pressure of a scream rose as Jonah slouched in the bathroom doorway, pinging the floss between his teeth. Your prince has turned into a frog, and the rising pond-stink permeates your sheets. The once crisp linen is soggy, the air muggy with discontent. Your princess curls have turned into wild witch's locks, and a curse, like a scorpion, blossoms on your tongue.

The man's jeans are crossed at the ankles. His feet twitch as if he is flicking away flies. Ghost flies, because he surely can't feel anything through all his clothing. His hand arcs up his side, under his ribs, down to his hips, scratching, scratching. He inspects his fingernails, scraping each with the opposite nail, one by one. He undoes his buckle. You stare, fascinated, rude. He redoes his belt, tighter, without exposing himself.

The waiter brings a latte, velvet froth curling over the rim. On the red bench, the man rolls up his garments, examining the insides, searching for something. Will he find a brittle label on the seam, a leaf shard stuck in the weave of his vest? A sharp twig?

Although the pavement is shimmering hot, he is wearing several layers. He peels them back, all the clothes he owns: a pale jacket showing the dirt, overshirts, shirts, undershirts. The creases on his stomach are visible from across the road. You think about Jonah, who sleeps turned away from you, curled up like a dog. If you leave him, will he come to this?

From his pocket, the man takes the paper and writes on it. He forms each letter with painstaking slowness, as if pricking out syllables with a seed husk. If you had a telephoto lens, you could capture the metre of the lines in his face. If you had a telescope, you'd see the nits in his belly hair hatching into nymphs, tan-coloured body lice, smaller than sesame seeds.

The waiter asks what you'll have to eat. You are hungry, but the menu is costly, and you can afford only one latte. You say you're fine; you would like water now, no ice. You finger your chipped crown, which is rough to the touch. You wonder how you will pay the dentist.

The waiter crosses the street, hands the man a hunk of bread, a carton of mageu. You watch as he tears the soft whiteness with both hands, filling his mouth, open and moist. When he drinks, hungrily and unashamed, you imagine he smells like dry grass and crushed leaves. You guess he tastes bitter like bluegums, sour as the veld. The ground will be even and unyielding beneath your knees when you lie with him in a nest of his vests, under a new moon.

Light years from home, when you start to itch, you'll remember everything you've forgotten you still love in Jonah. You'll thank the old man. You'll tell him he's your blessing.

Tease

The Science of Curves

"INTRODUCTION TO FRACTALS is intended for students without especially strong mathematical preparation, or any particular interest in science."

I stare at the outline of Dr Henderson's breasts as she turns from the board. Beneath the tight orange jersey, they are snug, so much smaller than my own.

"Fractal geometry offers a new way of looking at the world."

By mutual agreement, I don't question her in class. I do not need this credit; I simply want to observe my lover. I sit in front, noting how the cerise and aqua stripes on my socks swell and flatten as I flex my ankle.

"We are surrounded by natural patterns, usually un-recognised, unsuspected. Sensuous, irregular configur-ations occur in, and relate to, the arts, the humanities, the social sciences."

Her rounded buttocks sway as she walks to a window. Filtered light falls on her oval face. She throws the shutters open. Agitation flutters across her features.

"Examining the fractal curve, we see traces of complex dynamic systems self-organising into familiar natural shapes. Our understanding of the underlying mathematics enables us to model eroded coastlines, snowflakes, or the human vascular system, in which patterns recur on progressively smaller scales."

She ignores my gaze, hiding behind her notes on the lectern.

"The determinism of chaos describes partly random phenomena such as crystal growth…"

Last night she wrestled her wedding bands off over her bent finger, her mouth a guilty twist. I imagine a supersaturated sucrose solution crystallising around her diamond.

"… fluid turbulence…"

Bath oil capsules dissolved in pink swirls, releasing the scent of vetiver and honey into the steam.

"… and galaxy formation."

I unclipped her suspenders, peeled off her stockings, sucked her toes, kissed the arch of foot. Her pelvis rocked in the water. Afterwards she said, "I saw the stars, the planets. So lovely."

Christmas Eve Picnic, Pretoria

Under leafy jacaranda branches in our private garden, I wipe down the slatted picnic table I made for you last Christmas. I throw the embroidered cloth you stitched for me over it, and set two earthenware dishes on each side.

You place a round of Brie, pale as your breast, beside a salad of herbs, oven-baked bread, olives and pretty slivers of cold ham. I bring a sumptuous fruit bowl with summer jewels from the Cape: hanepoot grapes, fat as your nipple, fuzzy peaches, beautiful as your buttocks, watermelon, litchis, plums.

I wipe crumbs from your mouth after you've eaten, and we clear the table. I undo your ribbon ties, finger your buttons. Your foot slides up the bench, revealing you naked under your skirt. Your hairless flesh is pink as cherry blossoms, inner lips burgundy as the leaves on the prunus. Sandals off, you slip a toe under my shorts. You suck my finger. I run it slowly along your teeth.

139

My tongue in your ear, I say, "I want you where I want you."

"Eat me," you say.

"Greedy girl! You must wait." I place a gift on the table, telling you to open it.

Tomorrow I will carve a steaming turkey for your family; you will redden as you whip up the brandy butter my mother always praises. Your father will tell us how much he appreciates a traditional dinner. We will all know that what he would really like is a traditional wedding for his only daughter, but we will all let it pass because it's Christmas, and the new South Africa, and same-sex marriages are now constitutional.

My brother will look at your cleavage when he says, "Delicious!", and I will give him a look that says, "Don't even think it!"

Your uncle will stare at my low-slung jeans and say, "You girls, um, ladies, sure cook up a storm, don't you?" We will all laugh at the double entendre, and you will shift gingerly in your chair.

You will giggle over the Christmas pudding we both detest, remembering how I tied you to this sturdy table, how I sliced this mango above your belly. Your panties will moisten again, recalling how I dribbled juice from the knife blade down your cleft. You will blush to think of me licking this knife before tracing its point around your nipples – a preparatory gesture.

Tomorrow you will be glad that I'm giving you your Christmas present now, and not in front of our families. In a moment you will beg for the gag so the neighbours don't hear, because I'm going to test it out now, under the jacaranda trees: a heavy flogger made of old copper leather – the one you pointed out in the catalogue. I will refuse you the gag because you're no longer an initiate, you've learned control. You will contain your screams while I lash your thighs, your belly, your breasts. You will maintain silence afterwards as I slide the handle into your soaking cunt. You will hold your breath until lightning forks across the sky and a lilac blossom falls into the well of your navel. And only then, as your orgasm explodes, will you moan your release. Cradled in my arms again, you will weep your relief.

But you will cry again when you open your real present – which I will bring you on a tray with your morning coffee and croissant. I will throw open the shutters and the sun will stream in, shining on the gold wrapping paper you tear off the tiny box, glinting off the diamond you'll hold up in disbelief, sparkling a rainbow as I slide it onto your fourth finger.

Vanilla Silk

"Don't underestimate her." Madame Bettina's instant message flickered across my screen late on Monday afternoon. We were finalising the arrangements for my first corrective therapy session.

"Sarah's vanilla all the way," I typed back from my university office.

"Doesn't mean she's stupid."

"Sure."

"She hasn't guessed?"

"Nope."

On Tuesday, a plain manila envelope arrived in the mail. I opened the contract unwittingly at the kitchen table, in front of my wife. My stomach clutched.

Terms of our agreement… bound, gagged, caned… restraint shall not be removed… further correction required… The safe word "vanilla silk" will indicate…

Sarah stared at the envelope I held in trembling fingers.

I whisked it away, stammering a feeble lie.

"How pale you look," she said, stroking me with cool hands. I caught a whiff of Happy, the sweet perfume she preferred. I'd given her Dior's Poison, but she refused to wear it. "Too dark," she'd said.

Thursday's package contained a leather blindfold and six-inch heels. I blushed at the ivory lace thong, cream stockings and twelve-clip suspender belt. My legs bounced in uncontrollable agitation, my erection throbbed.

Undressing to meet my Mistress, I yearned momentarily to flee, to return to the safety of Sarah's toasted cheese sandwiches and our safe, seemingly happy home. But once I'd slid my foot into the hose and adjusted the seams, I couldn't go back. A floral motif on the ankle matched the lace tops where the garters attached. I felt nauseous with anxiety, demented with desire. My dick swelled against the lace as I slipped the blindfold on and waited as instructed.

My back to the door, arms behind me, I dared not turn towards her footsteps. I surrendered to the click of handcuffs.

As she opened my mouth to put in the rubber gag, an ominous whiff of Poison filled the room.

"How pale you look," she said.

State Theatre

It is Saturday in the State Theatre, and there's just enough time between the matinée and the evening shows of *My Fair Lady* to grab a sandwich. I used to be able to leave my bassoon in the pit, but instruments get stolen these days. It's too heavy to schlep around, so I hide the bassoon case in the shower stall in the change rooms.

Nobody showers here any more. Nobody even comes here. In the old days, there were pale ballerinas with pointy bones and blank faces. We, the orchestra girls, would bustle past them in the shared amenity, feeling enormous. I was pregnant and the biggest of all. My borrowed black maternity shift cut into my armpits; I was always plucking at the sleeves. When I refreshed my lipstick at the mirror, I'd peep sideways as the ballerinas peeled off their leg warmers and leotards, envious of their flat stomachs and spidery limbs.

In the canteen, they used to buy apples and cigarettes. I'd order a hamburger and *slap* chips, blushing privately as I scraped up my prenatal entitlement. And when I lugged the contrabassoon into the pit, I felt as unbecoming as my cumbersome instrument. I hated its rude sound, like fat vibrating farts. Eating before I played gave me acid reflux.

When my baby was born I couldn't hear anything except his cries in my head, raucous as the hadeda ibis at dawn. In rehearsals I'd count the rests, take up my instrument, inhale, watch the conductor, play a note and wince. Too sharp. Or flat? I'd pinch my lips, bite harder. My principal would scowl. I'd shake, lose my place, mess up the key changes, miss entries.

After my last performance, I drove the hour home at midnight with full breasts, hoping my baby would feed. Walt Ledbetter growled on my radio: "My girl, my girl, don't you lie to me. Tell me, where did you sleep last night?" At home in the shower, my milk swirled, bluish, down the drain.

The next day I phoned the booker and said I'd call him once the baby was sleeping through the night. Then the orchestra closed down. It was 1994, and the new South Africa didn't want white men's music any more.

Twelve years later we're back, but the theatre looks shabby, with graffiti and broken soap dispensers. You have to bring your own toilet paper. The dancers are black girls now, hip-hopping in the lifts – robust, with hips and breasts and attitude. They eat Big Macs and their cell phones have kwaito ring tones, which they answer like American TV stars, shoulders swaying, fingers snapping.

In the pit, before the performance, the tall clarinet player beside me tucks one foot under his hugely muscled thigh and sucks his reed. His head is thrown back, eyes closed. I study his face, close enough to touch: receding hairline, full lips. I want to reach under the clarinet shielded against his chest, to feel his pecs, his abs. Instead, I practise the tricky solo in "Why Can't The English?" The clarinet player opens his eyes and says, "That one's a dog; try it slower." I do.

During the clarinet solo, I observe his construction-worker's fingers moving over the keys. He catches me watching him and winks. I blush, imagining his fingertips on my collarbone, on my chin, moving lower. I want him to make me croon sweeter than his clarinet. I count the measures until my solo, wanting to kiss the fleshy pad of his thumb. He nods, offering me the cue. We breathe together and blow. His note above, mine bass to the chord. Later, when I play my own solo, the sound is pure and true. The clarinet player scrapes his foot on the floor, orchestra code for "well done".

On Sunday after the matinée, I will follow Mr Clarinet out the pit, whistling "Wouldn't It Be Luverly?" I'll follow him to the canteen, then join him at a rickety table and sip a coffee while he rips the flesh off a chicken drumstick, imagining myself bold enough to lure him to my hiding place in the shower.

What You Really Need

Jim lounges beside me against the counter in crinkled chinos and a crisp denim shirt.

"Tired?" I ask.

"A little shopping goes a long way," he says, slipping his veined hand under my sleeveless blouse. He teases my bra strap, plucking and releasing it.

"We're nearly done. This is the last item on the Christmas shopping list."

The clerk who giftwraps the embroidered towels I have chosen for our eldest granddaughter looks about the same age as her. The girl strokes the peach satin monogram before cutting a length of red-and-green paper. There is a tiny engagement ring on her finger, a wistful look on her face.

"Pretty," I say.

"Nice and absorbent," she says.

"I meant your ring."

"Oh, thanks," she laughs, holding the ring out momentarily for me to admire, before creasing the paper into an elaborate design. Cutting tape, she flicks it in place with swift fingertips.

I wonder if she has ever shared a bathtub with her fiancé. I hope he folds her in sumptuous towels afterwards, rubs her softly and unwraps her tenderly.

My eyes rest on Jim's crotch. He catches my indiscreet stare, twirls his hand through my short curls, and wraps a lock around his forefinger. It is a proprietorial gesture. He gives a sharp tug, a private signal.

"So, when's the big day?" I look up.

"April 12th." She snips a strand of silver ribbon.

"Nice! We had an autumn wedding, didn't we?" I prod Jim's tummy. He nods and smiles. The girl blushes. She deftly twists a many-looped bow. I wish this girl glorious weather, a beautiful ceremony, and a long, happy marriage. If her groom is half as gentle between the sheets, half as patient on the pillow as my blue-eyed lavender-tipped boy, she will be a contented bride. If her husband has anything like Jim's strong arm, his judicious eye for the correct position of the paddle, if he knows when to use a riding crop and when to use his own bare hand, she will grow to be a deeply satisfied old woman.

"Merry Christmas," she says, handing Jim the parcel.

"You too," he smiles.

"Have a nice wedding," I say.

After we've gone, I think about what I should have said. I wish I had whispered in her ear, "Show him what you like. Ask for what you want. Don't be afraid to tell him what you really need."

The Exact Location
of the Exit

in memory of Walter Mony

The Heat is On
1pm, 10 February 2007, Blairgowrie, Johannesburg

WHEN WE BOUGHT the house in Blairgowrie a year ago, I wanted to fill in the pool. The fibreglass layered over the old concrete shell looks even shabbier now, and attracts black mould in clumps in the summer. Tim still wants to redo it, and has set aside savings for the repairs. But I have other plans for the money.

Steam rises off the slasto, gravy-coloured and chipped. Its flaky edge is softened by the phygelius that blooms in clusters. We planted indigenous, wanting to save water. The guy at the garden centre said this was a "robust plant that occurs naturally along rocky stream banks in open woodland at altitudes up to 2000 metres". He spoke as if he'd memorised a textbook.

When we bought the house I thought it would be forever, but in a few minutes, I will rinse off the chlorine, dry myself, and dress for the Toronto winter. In five days, I will open a bank account at the Royal Bank of Canada. Twelve years after democracy we are still fat white babies, unable to swim. Our water wings have cracks where the rubber has perished.

Cleave

2pm, 10 February 2007, Oliver Tambo International Airport
Tim parks in a kiss-and-fly bay at the airport. Despite the shriek and bustle, traffic cops blink slowly in the sun that has just begun to slant from the west.

A woman yelling into her cell phone gesticulates at the officers. Maybe her car has been towed. I triple-check my documents, harried by the sharp plastic folder that has sliced my finger. I suck the red pearls forming along the cut and remember my earrings beside my bed. What else did I forget?

Tim, who has been listening to the fracas, tells me the woman's car has been stolen. "From the secure parking." Our last hug is quick and uncomfortable. I haven't told him and he hasn't asked why I'm really travelling. He's heard about the conferences, the panel discussion, the reading. He believes I'm networking. He says, "Have a good time. Send my best to Ann and Walter." Our former Professor of Music has insisted I visit him en route to the States. "You have to get out of here," he said, when he stayed with us in December. "Come to Canada," he said, "at least come for a look."

Before leaving I grab Tim's hand one last time, holding it hard, reluctant to leave. His skin, as always, is cool and dry.

Dressing

2:10pm, 10 February 2007, Oliver Tambo International Airport Departure Lounge
A toddler waving an ice cream darts from the tightly gathered Muslim clan and into my path. Before we collide he is caught by a youth, made more lanky by his high fez. Despite the malfunctioning air conditioning, the women in their long black layers seem unperturbed. Why don't they

wear white like their men? Their eyes give away nothing through the tiny slits in the fabric.

My palms sweat as I pass my laptop into the X-ray machine and I'm regretting the buttered muffin that's burning a path back up my oesophagus. The Emirates cabin crew walk past, laughing and chattering in their burgundy caps with veils. They sway, bird-like, on their heels. I'm wearing a new yellow skirt for the first time – a mistake. The corduroy clings and the label bristles in the small of my back.

We are ushered onto the plane an hour before take-off. I squeeze into the narrow lavatory before noticing a puddle on the floor. I roll up the skirt's bulky fabric, tucking the hem firmly about my middle. I need one hand to keep the lavatory seat down, another for the lid that won't stay up. Now how do I remove my stockings? I exit in search of better plumbing.

Back at my seat, glad not to be wearing a hijab, I squat to reach my book, which has slipped below the seat, and a seam splits at my knee. As I straighten, I stand on the hem. Stitches pop underfoot.

Icy

1pm, 11 February 2007, Washington Dulles Airport

The South Africans are audible from a long way off. "There should be a direct flight to Toronto. Jeez, such a long stop in Dakar. Ja, honestly. Seventeen hours from Jozi and now this… Air Canada should get with the programme."

My parents always avoided other South Africans when they travelled. Now I too want to be as far away as possible from my compatriots. Do I also sound so whiny, so hard done by?

A black woman from the South African contingent sits alone in the row ahead of me. A white guy with a balding head says "Sawubona" as he approaches. She sniffs, but he doesn't seem to notice. She probably doesn't speak the language. I think I detect her irritation at his assumption that Zulu flows from every black South African's mouth. She replies in Xhosa, but the shift is too subtle and he doesn't pick it up.

"So where you from, hey?" His nasal drawl identifies him as Joburg Jewish.

"South Africa," she replies.

"Thekwini?" He uses the Zulu name for Durban and mispronounces it.

"East London," she says in a chilly tone.

I slump in my seat, wincing with recognition. His misguided attempt at friendliness is the sort of sanctimonious nationalism of which I'm equally capable if I find myself feeling isolated.

Why do whites feel compelled to show off their three phrases of ill-pronounced Zulu learned from TV commercials to any black person who will listen? Do we still yearn for the nannies that once carried us on their backs, clapping their hands and singing our praises?

On the flight, I dream that great patches of my legs turn black and form scabs. When I peel them off they are dry and dusty, like tree bark. Underneath, my flesh has turned to compost, like powdery tea leaves. I brush away the dead stuff, down to the bone where the membrane is clear as glass and tender as a burn. The blood flowing through my veins is no longer red. It has turned black. Now I have a black heart, too.

"Cabin crew, please prepare for descent." From the air, the flat scenery glistens. I wasn't expecting rain somehow. "On arrival the temperature will be minus nine degrees." What does that mean? Leaning closer to the window, I bump my nose. The only snow I know in

South Africa appears discreetly on rural mountaintops, the Drakensberg, Hottentots' Holland. I've seen it on TV.

"So much snow," I say to the black woman whose eye contact has granted permission for conversation. She is headed for Ottawa, where "real" snow falls ten feet at a time. "This," she says, dismissing Toronto, "is nothing."

We enter the airport together and wait for our suitcases at the carousel. She introduces herself as Lilly Jane. "This place is so amazing," I say, waving at the space, wanton in its excess. The architectural lines are streamlined and luxurious, letting in the light as if there were no shortage. "Everything is so open, so clean."

She says, "Canada is the cleanest place on earth. I want to bring everyone from home here for just one day. Then they'd know the meaning of clean."

Accent
1pm, 12 February 2007, Woodstock, Ontario

People say "puffs", but I hear "puss"; they say "aunty", I hear "anti". Jazzy describes a kid in her class who is "as backward". I ponder the odd construction for a while before asking, "As backward as what?"

"Ass backward," she laughs. Arse backward. Like me.

Brian, her dad, a retired schoolteacher, cooks and keeps house, making lasagne from scratch and pizza with peppers. He bakes bread. That's not backward in anyone's language.

Brian tells me his daughter plays basketball for the Native team.

"Did you say na…?" I ask. The reluctant word, so long a negation, sticks in my throat.

"Sure," says Brian, who married a woman on the Reservation in the far north, "Jazzy is Native."

In the mornings, he shovels the path clear of "hard

attack snow". In the afternoons, he drives her to a match in another city two hours away. Two hours? "That's nothing," he says. "In the spring break, we'll drive across the country to visit Jazzy's mother."

Is Brian accommodating because he's my father's age? An "older" dad, an "elder"? Is it a Canadian thing? Is it "Native"? Because he's a single father? Back in Johannesburg, I will be a good mother to my children. I will "cook healthy" and attend their regattas.

But Gauteng drivers intimidate me with their speed and rude hand signs, and Roodeplaat Dam is ninety minutes away. Just a jump by Canadian standards, but South Africans don't drive like Canadians. The highway takes force.

At my daughter's races, I'm reluctant to sit with the parents who drive big Jeeps with loud hooters. Their designer camping chairs and coolers stuffed with beer and grilled chicken bespeak "money" and "order". I'm retiring when they greet me, their voices rising an octave. Their friendly offers of coffee are concealed invitations to gossip: "Her daughter cuts. Her daughter is too thin."

Next time I'm there, I won't be cowed. I will take out my laptop and assume a busy mien. When another mother asks what I'm up to, I'll tell her I'm riding.

"Writing?" she'll ask, and I'll say "yeah" instead of "ja".

Spillage
1-ish, 15 February 2007, Sidney-by-the-Sea, British Columbia
Ann and I walk along the jetty extending out into the dark water of the Strait of Juan de Fuca. Does this ocean ever get warm enough for swimming? The Olympic Mountains, a lighter shade of grey, loom in the distance.

Along the promenade we meet Ann's friend, who wants to rest her bunions. She invites us to join her for a bite.

"Lunchtime," says Ann. But it can't be. It seems much later. The overcast light is muted, like dusk. My watch and body are still on Joburg time, where it's the middle of the night and I'm not hungry.

While we wait for our table, the Canadian lady says, "Isn't South Africa the most beautiful spot on earth? I'd love to visit your wonderful country."

Ann says, "No, you wouldn't. I wouldn't go back if you paid me." A giant halibut mounted on the wall surveys the nautical scene.

"So how is Nelson Mandela getting along?"

"Getting old," says Ann.

"Do you see him out and about?"

Ann rolls her eyes and says, "Oh, please." And then, "You haven't been at jewellery-making lately. Have you switched to the other class?"

"Here, take the ocean view," Ann's friend says to me as we are seated. It would be rude to refuse, but I prefer to see the door. I'm not acclimatised to the calm here yet, and I keep swivelling, seeking the exact location of the exit.

"Are you looking for something, dear?" asks the Canadian lady. I can't explain my door obsession, can't describe how the mere click of a ballpoint pen can muscle open a too recently sealed vault. Two years earlier, a view of the door afforded me a momentary advantage when six armed men entered the living room. I saw them before they saw me. I wrenched off my diamond rings, slipped them into my mouth, and kicked my handbag out of sight under the couch, but I forgot not to look. The leader of the gang met my eye and said, "Kill them all."

When Ann steps out to the restroom, the woman presses me again about home. I pick an oozing hangnail on my thumb, and mention the Chief of Police who went shopping for Armani suits with his drug-lord pal, the one who was charged with the murder of Brett Kebble. I talk about the laser beams we installed because the razor wire wasn't enough, the expense of it, the relentless jitters. "The beams are troublesome, giving false alarms when the hadedas fly in to land, and sometimes the security company can take twenty minutes to respond," I say. "That's a long time if you're being raped at gunpoint."

The Canadian lady's eyes widen. "A teacher's wife was raped in their home on St John's College campus, what with all their fancy security." My tone rises as I jabber on about babies violated for mythical cures. She rests her knife meticulously between the tines of her fork. She's had enough. But I can't stop speaking about cash-in-transit heists carried out with military precision, the ambushes on the highway, guards trapped in their armoured cars burning alive. I shouldn't be bad-mouthing my country, yet I can't stop talkingtalkingtalking about Aids orphans and child-headed households. She pats her lips with the napkin, wanting silence, but I say, "I read in the *Mail & Guardian* on the plane about old women hiding their pension in their vaginas. Now when these grandmothers are robbed, their most private cavities are routinely invaded."

Ann, just back, her pale lipstick reapplied, harrumphs into her seat. "See I told you: it's a terrible place."

I say, "I'm sorry, so sorry." I've spoilt the lunch now. Poor form. So rude. I should have spoken of lovely things – baby elephants, the game parks. Daisies in Namaqualand, Kirstenbosch in spring.

Stretching for the pepper, my arm bumps against my bowl. The halibut's glass eye watches the soup as it slops over the edge and lands steaming in my lap.

House Guest

1am, 16 February 2007, Brentwood Bay, British Columbia

My sleep spirals out to other planes as my body stays grounded on Central African Time. I nap for an hour, wake for three. My skin is too tight for the new longing that pumps in my veins. A yearning for outrageous possibilities flares and then twists in my gut.

I text my sister in Joburg in the middle of the night to tell her I'm smitten. Canada is my new lover, and I'm hot for its touch. Even the toilets flush exuberantly. In the middle of the night, it's an outburst of delight. Or a prank that wakes whoever is sleeping.

As I pad back to bed, Walter and Ann mumble in the room above. What do old people talk of after fifty years together? Do they still make love? The dog is let out. A tap runs and the drain gurgles. Their bedsprings creak and fall silent. Soon their snores are a duet, accompanied by the purring heat vent, a permanent white noise. No barking penetrates the double glazing. There are no squalling night birds, no tick-tick-tick of an electric fence. Canadians are discreet with their functional picket fences. They keep small dogs that sleep inside all winter and are safe in back yards in summer.

I dream I have a new cell phone, ice-white and pretty, with a dial but no instruction manual. I can't figure how it works, and can't call home. I am sleeping in a hotel room and friendly old people stand around my bed. I'm crying in my sleep, but the old people can't wake me.

When I wake in Ann and Walter's spare room, my face is wet. I open the window a sliver and reach into the chilly air with a hand that is milky in the streetlight.

Are there really no burglars here? And if they do come, what warning do they give? What do they steal? Walter's hosepipe stays on the verge each morning where he left it.

The deckchairs never walk. I text my sister: *I don't want to leave.*

We will live here, in this place where sirens don't slice open the night, and the only sound is the erratic patter of dripping branches.

Under the duvet, I warm my icy hand between my thighs, waiting once again for sleep. But I can't settle because with the window closed, I can't hear the rain.

Devotions to Divine Mercy
10am, 17 February 2007, Victoria, British Columbia

Walter drops me off in Quadra Street on his way to the Conservatory. I step into a puddle that stretches across the road while he says, "Go to the Bay when you're hungry. You can eat for under $10 because it's subsidised. It's on the fifth floor. Sit at the window, where you can see the aquaplanes coming in. Get there early, before the good stuff is gone."

I skim the notice board at the back of the cathedral, reading the bulletins, the schedule for worship: Mass, Rosary, Eucharistic Adoration. The light from stained-glass windows falls across the benches. Beneath St Cecilia playing the organ I finger a leaflet, forgetting how to pray. I neglect to adjust the settings on my camera and when the flash explodes, I feel I've intruded.

In the street I watch people walking past, certain I won't bump into anyone familiar. I'm not sure how I feel about being so completely alone. Nobody makes eye contact, except for a Sikh taxi driver and the aimless, lingering homeless.

Who is the outsider in Victoria? Where is the foreigner? Not the Natives – Walter assures me they are called First Nation. There are a few Asians, but almost everybody is Caucasian. No black faces. Even the street people look like me.

A youth in a rat-coloured hoodie with pale dreads crosses the road towards me, his eyes on mine. He walks right at me. Too close. I step left as he steps to his right. I step right. He steps left. Adrenaline surges. Time slows. Bad teeth, clear skin. His eyes bore through me. Like another time. The leader of the gang saw me. The youth raises his eyebrows, surprised by something new. Not disgust or pity, a different response. I can't hold the gaze. I couldn't before. Then, I dropped my eyes instinctively. This time I lower them in shame – burning because my terror has been seen. I walk on, looking down, noticing the dark leather of my wet shoes.

The totem pole honouring Canadian aboriginal war veterans stands on a promontory near the ocean, looking out to sea. I circle it slowly, then move in close, staring upwards until I feel dizzy. At the water's edge, I hold out my hands for the spray's benediction. I mumble "Thy will be done," unsure of which deity I've addressed.

Before I leave, I spit in the sea.

Landing on Water
1pm, 17 February 2007, The Bay, Victoria, British Columbia

The multistorey shopping mall consumes a whole block. Inside it, the ladies' room is the size of a plot, and dazzling fluorescent lights reveal neither chipped tiles nor rickety fixtures. I absorb the sparkle, the meaning of clean.

The great whooshing vortex of the automatic flush startles me as I stand. When I hold out my hands at the basin, the spout also gushes of its own accord. I think I like it, this anticipation of my needs delivered with mechanical precision. Inspired plumbing has a charm of its own.

I open my palm beneath the soap dispenser. Nothing. Wave my hand to activate the invisible beam. Nothing. At the next sink, a silver-haired woman pumps the spout with good old-fashioned vigour. I try not to stare like a bumpkin. Older than my mother, she's soon joined by a trio of other seventy-somethings, applying lip colour and lotion.

With elderly folk about, a place feels safe. Their presence indicates something wholesome in a society, clean water, safe air, pavements swept clear of snow. Wherever I go, there they are. Undaunted by the weather, they walk their dogs and volunteer at the library, tootling along in motorised carts to visit their friends.

I follow the women out of the bathroom and along to the elevator, where one of them presses the button with flair. They're all going somewhere together, Joyce, Maud, Jane and one whose name I don't catch. I listen to their small talk, observing the quality details of their clothing, their sturdy but stylish shoes. I'm intrigued by their lack of fear. My imagination is on fire: here is where I want to grow old.

When we step into the elevator together, they smile and greet. I redden, imagining that they've observed my bold study of their longevity. When the elevator stops at the top, we all get out. Walter said to go to the fifth floor, but we're on the fourth. I look for another elevator, a flight of stairs. Nothing obvious, and nobody appears hungry. No smells offering clues, so where to from here? I run after Maud, disappearing around a corner. She gestures down a corridor and waves me goodbye.

The passage is long and lined with empty shops. "Rent this space" signs appear in each window. Could I open a shop in the Bay to keep us going? How hard is it to run a business, anyway? When I find the food court, it has the universal chicken joint, chip shop and pizza parlour. Like Sandton City, but with better furniture. The view is of a lattice trellis and the empty pots of a winter-dead balcony, not aquaplanes arriving from Seattle. In June, it will bloom with flowers so brilliantly coloured that those who don't know better will tweak the blossoms, checking if they're real.

Eventually, an escalator going up another level deposits me below two arrows pointing in opposite directions to the Harbor Café. This must be the place that Walter recommended, but which arrow to follow? Are there two cafés? I traipse through the towels and comforters of the linen department, but arrive back at the gift register, where the arrows still point in opposite directions. I have to do it; I must ask for help.

At the Harbor Café, I can't figure out the currency exchange, but the bean soup with a mini-loaf looks comforting. I have to ask again: which is the cup, which the bowl. One is bigger. One has a handle. The $5.29 option comes with bread; the $5.99 one includes a cheese biscuit. There are no crackers and I see no cheese, but the attendant points out a savoury scone, explaining once again.

At the beverage counter, a pensioner selects from the tea display: raspberry, green tea, mint and jasmine. He fills his pot with shaky hands. No one sighs when he messes; nobody clicks their tongue. A thermos labelled chocolate stands in a row of similar air pots with fanciful names: French vanilla, Irish cream, noisette and cinnamon pastry.

Again I'm forced to ask, "Is the hot chocolate extra?"

"It's a blend." Blend, that's what I'll have to learn to do.

"A coffee blend?"

"Yes ma'am, part of the deal."

I'm shaky at the cashier, afraid of dropping my tray. I can't tell a nickel from a dime, and hold open my fist of coins. She picks out what I owe. I swipe at a grateful tear threatening to start a downfall. This is soup, I tell myself, not some unpronounceable mystery. The women in headscarves speaking Arabic at the airport face a real challenge. By comparison, I blend right in. Don't even need to revive my matric French. So what exactly is my problem?

The mini-loaf in my hand feels too light. The butter fractures and won't spread. Suddenly, I'm missing Spar's heavy seed-loaf that I know and trust. Bread is not something to cry over. Breathe and chew. If Ann could leave Joburg at seventy, it'll be a cinch for me at forty.

The city rooftops are covered in grass. What oddness. I remember postcards in primary school, sent from a girl who went to Norway. Do they keep goats up here to keep it short?

It's moss. Not grass. This isn't the patchy lichen that grows on rooftops in Durban. It's a dense velvet caution, warning of ten long months of cold and wet. Ponder that, I tell myself, before moving to the land of the tumble-dryer.

Somewhere over Africa
Time to go home, 4 March 2007, SA 207, 63D
I do the algebra of the sleep equation from my window seat. Three weeks, seven cities, prolonged insomnia and a dinky of wine. A single sleeping tablet and a teal SAA blanket will take me out for the last fifteen-hour stretch.

I'm cowering in a desert storm wearing heavy veils, grateful for the protection against the stinging red sand whipped by the wind. But it's not a dust storm. The mandibles of a million locusts are tugging at the threads of my clothing. They bite through the fabric, strip me and leave me exposed. As they fly off, a sandstorm of rocks rises, whirling shards and sharp stones that rip away my flesh. When the wind dies down, all that remains is my naked pile of bones, porous and bleached against the rust-red sand.

I wake sweating and itchy, fretting about bedbugs. The flight attendant brings water and orange juice. I drink quickly and ask for more. I dismiss my discomfort as dry skin, the result of the punishing ventilation pumping through the cabin, and try the hand cream in the dispenser inside the toilet. It is highly perfumed and antagonises the itch.

The plane drops down through the high cumulonimbus that promises a traditional Highveld storm. The fences are pervasive, prominent but flimsy barriers between arbitrary boxed spaces. A thousand swimming pools whizz by in the Johannesburg suburbs below, no two the same. The shadow of the aeroplane flits across their odd shapes, lozenges and kidneys, edges rigid and round. St John's College, the Hillbrow Tower, the observatory and Wemmer Pan, where my daughter's last regatta was held, all pass beneath me.

Somewhere down there is the space I will re-inhabit and soon prepare to leave, a place where the mouldy swimming pool that Tim wants to renovate is a curious, blinking eye looking back up at me.

After the plane has landed, the steward, greeting each first-class passenger by name, makes small talk in the gaps between coats and carry-on bags. He says, "There's home, hey. Like no place."

Control
1:30pm, 5 March 2007, Oliver Tambo International Airport
I slide my documents across the counter and say, "Good afternoon, I'm home." No eye contact. No greeting. No chitchat. Ms Maluse in her brown Home Affairs uniform looks at my passport, but not at me. Did I speak too softly? Should I greet again, more loudly? No. It would sound like a rebuke.

Have I offended her with the suggestion that South Africa is my home? My French Huguenot ancestors arrived in the 1600s. The footprints of her ancestors exist as fossils, if one knows where to look. Ms Maluse doesn't give a fig. Her attention is on the hunk in the next booth. She slaps my passport back on the counter. I wait to be dismissed. No fingerprints? No questions? She signals to the next person, and inspects her French nails. They're losing their whiteness.

The heat is overpowering. Still no air conditioning. Olivia Newton-John is singing "Hopelessly devoted to you" as I roll my suitcase out to find Tim. Being back in Johannesburg is like the last days of my marriage, unable to leave, waiting to be hit. I hold Tim's hand, but what I have to tell him will need good timing. We walk in silence to the car, kissing every few steps.

At the exit of the secure parking, steel spines rise out of the ground to shred your tyres in case you try to tailgate without paying. The first billboard on the highway proffers an advertisement for tyres: "Run on flat. The tyre a puncture won't stop!"

A minibus taxi cuts in front of us, zaps into the next lane and up the off-ramp. The name it sports in a red Gothic font is "Slow Poison".

Home, Sick
All night long, 6 March 2007, Blairgowrie
In the heat, my ribs creak and my head throbs. Although the overhead fan shifts the air about, it makes no difference to the humidity. Nina Simone's "Ne me quittez pas" on my iPod exacerbates the temperature, but I cannot cry. My body has bitten the arms off its own clock. Without a face, I can't even sip water.

Tim turns over, resting his skinny buttocks against my

knees. I reach for his bald patch. The hair around it has grown thicker and more wiry since turning grey. Once it was fine and soft. He stirs and says, "I missed you." When I kiss his neck, he sighs and says, "Glad you're back." I wish I could say the same. The iPod slips off the bed, leaving the headphones dangling. With the music silenced, the fan claims my focus; its mild-mannered clattering is like a wire brush on a drum.

I remember that clean place where old people drink tea unafraid. I yearn for Tim Hortons on Dundas Street; I want to watch snowflakes beautify the sludge through a double-glazed window. I wish to feel safe and insulated.

I seek out a cool spot on the sheet that is crisp from sun-drying. Something hard and dry rests against my calf. A beetle carcass, maybe? Not brittle enough. Perhaps a spider? By the light of my cell phone, I discover a dried plumbago blossom from the hedge by the washing line. I'm back in Ann's basement, feeding my sorry yellow skirt into the Speed Queen, and I'm falling down a well of something like homesickness.

In the dark, padding on flat feet, I avoid the loosened parquet tiles that crackle underfoot, restless and exhausted. I must tell Tim I am leaving. I have to go back to Canada and take my children. Not for a visit next time, but for good. The burglar alarm goes off when, wanting tea, I forget to disarm it. Armed Response calls. I answer, apologising. If I leave, will Tim follow?

In the bathroom I tweeze tears from my eyelids, extracting them like slivers of quartz. They are brittle and shiny as flakes of mica, and smell of chlorine. I drop them in the small black box in which the jeweller wrapped my wedding band. The box fills and expands, the size of a tissue box, an apple box. I keep dropping the tears into the box. Opaque as rock salt, they come faster. I discard the tweezers, letting them fall straight into the box that continues to get bigger. It's the size of a car, a house, an aeroplane hangar. The door bursts open and my tears scatter on the wind, forming clumps on elders and maples, and drifting into banks of glittering crystals.

Tim shakes me awake. My body aches. His hand on my forehead is cool and dry. "You're burning up. Did you catch a bug on the plane?"

"Snowburn," I say.

"You were crying in your sleep."

Practice

IT IS WEDNESDAY, and I have still not begun the review of Shin Yu Pai's inscrutable *Adamantine*, which I promised two months ago. I carry her poetry in my handbag wherever I go, diving into it in the doctor's waiting room, probing each line, deciphering a world so unfamiliar that I fear I might never emerge from it. On the cover, now dog-eared, a stark and monumental hand thrusts up through the wastelands of the Atacama Desert.

Try as I might, no words of my own arrive to bring it home for another reader. I receive an email from the poet, asking after my son: has he made a good recovery? She asks whether I have managed to place my review. I pluck at the dried edge of a blister on my palm. I went too far in yesterday's training session. I needed the distance.

It is Wednesday, and in just one week I am scheduled to play bassoon again in a Mozart recital, co-principal to my first teacher, the man who taught me how to put the bassoon together, how to adjust the neck strap, how to soak a reed. A man who had a tic like a tortoise putting out its beak, retracting it back. I unpack my bassoon for the first time in nine months. Long enough to have borne a child. The wrappings on my bassoon reeds have loosened, the blades slip and twist.

It is Wednesday, and my son asks me to look into his eye, the eye that sometimes follows its brother, but mostly looks off to one side, blind. He complains of pain. "It feels like sand got in." How can a blind eye hurt? I am waiting for the doctor to call with test results.

It is Thursday, and I cannot answer Shin Yu Pai's email. I can't relate to her practice, so much deeper, so much more articulate than my own. I read "I Am Not Ready To Let Go" and wonder if I will ever be ready to hold on. It is unnecessary to close off the entire opening of the reed to articulate.

It is Thursday, and my bassoon rattles through the Milde études, squawky and irregular. My maiden name on the cover is printed in a schoolgirl's hand, a schoolgirl who knew only that she wanted to play in an orchestra, wanted it enough to change from the flute, which she loved, to the bassoon, which she did not, because there weren't enough bassoonists in town. Of flautists, there was a glut.

It is Thursday, and my son slouches into my room and flops on my bed. "Mama, cuddle me," he says, like a toddler. I say, "I'm busy. I have a review to write." He says, "Mama, Mama. You have to have to." I climb back onto my bed, spooning him, singing "Three Little Birds" like I did when he was five and came to my house only on weekends. *'Cos every little thing's gonna be alright…*

I remember my teacher talking about tonguing, explaining, "It is unnecessary to move the entire tongue in a back-to-front motion. Just the tip," he'd say, "the tip against the lower teeth."

It is Friday, and I put Shin Yu Pai at the top of my to-do list. Again. I go online, researching optimal productivity, registering at teuxdeax.com before de-registering and signing up for rememberthemilk.com instead. I horse around on the net, researching bassoon vacancies, studying audition lists. I can't stop procrastinating. I'm not even woolgathering. I get tips on tonguing the fast passages, the Beethoven fourth solo. I attend a cyber-masterclass: The tongue's upper surface, behind the tip of the tongue, comes into contact with the edge of the bottom blade.

It is Friday, and I drive to the city to meet my old bassoon teacher. He has prepared me a reed. My phone rings as I step inside his house. I gesture apologetically, mouth "the doctor". He overhears me asking the meaning of "central events". He hears me say, "The brain fails to signal the muscles to breathe?" I try some scales, which remain in my fingers. Uneven and unsteady, but lodged there as a body memory. My teacher's tic, which once intruded in every lesson, is barely present. He says he will pray for me, will pray for my son. He tells me he himself has been restored to health: "God answers prayer." Thanking him, I say, "I know."

It is Friday, the end of the summer holidays. I ask my son's father to call him, to explain this thing beyond comprehension. His father lives in Johannesburg, but they are close. His father is good at explaining things. After the call, we look it up on the internet, immediately regretting it. On the first website we read: *Brainstem dysfunction that leads to central sleep apnoea may be due to brain tumours.* On the second: *Central sleep apnoea often occurs in people who have certain medical conditions. For example, it can develop in persons who have life-threatening problems with the brainstem.*

It is Saturday, and I ignore Shin Yu Pai's email, but not her book. A pinhole of understanding opens in "Hozho", with its words scattered over a double page like a trail of bread crumbs, words that create *a basis for/ belief in/ the collapse of/ meaning/ into the intimate and the vast.*

It is Saturday, and my son starts eleventh grade on Monday. Every year there were surgeries. Some minor, like infected toenails, like a hernia popped. Some major, like a tumour, like a detached retina. He says, "Mama, I'm hungry." I say, "You're a big lad and the fridge is full. Go get yourself a plate of what you fancy." He slumps and says, "Mama, I'm too hungry to sleep, too tired to eat."

I slice a banana, shake cinnamon over yoghurt, drizzle it with honey. Like I did when he was little, I spoon it into his mouth. We watch a video on YouTube together of the *British Medical Journal*'s findings: that moderate cases of obstructive sleep apnoea improve with regular practice of the didgeridoo.

It is Saturday, and I blow long notes that waver off-key just under pitch, long notes I am powerless to raise. There's no bulge to my tongue, my lips run slack.

It is Sunday, a windless morning. I take the single scull out, and a set of cleavers. I row past Pelican Point where my son showed me balance exercises last summer. I go on round to the weir, back past the island and into Home Bay. I promise to email Shin Yu Pai afterwards, when the wind picks up. She wrote "Thirteen Ways of Looking at a Vulture". I will write "Thirteen Ways of Looking at a Surgeon".

It is Sunday, and my son returns from church. Who will spit on the ground and make clay with saliva? Who will anoint his eye and say, "Go, wash in the pool of Siloam," so that he might return to seeing?

It is Sunday, and I soak my reed in a glass of water. I open the score of the Mozart clarinet concerto, remembering the rapid staccato passages. My tongue is sluggish, the reed too hard. It cuts into my lower lip, leaving ridges where my teeth pressure from below. I have no heart for pain today.

My teacher warned me that the tongue slows down as one ages.

It is Monday, and the editor emails enquiring when the promised review might arrive. Her deadline is Wednesday. I say, "You'll have it tonight." It will please Shin Yu Pai, and I will not be ashamed that I did not sing the praises of her tender "Search & Recovery".

It is Monday, and the doctor calls, informing me that he

has written the motivation for a magnetic resonance image, a brain scan. Tomorrow at the hospital. Today, though, I collect my son after school and drive to the mall. We fetch his laptop booked in last week for repair. The technician regrets that it is still not ready. He couldn't perform the requested hard-drive upgrade. As we leave the store, I tousle the hair at the back of his neck, cut short for school. I wonder about that rugby concussion. Could that be the cause?

It is Monday, and too late to practise without inconveniencing the neighbours. Two days now, the bassoon has stood untouched in the corner by the piano.

In the end notes of *Adamantine*, I read that "Hozho" refers to the Navajo word for beauty, balance, harmony – "and the effort towards".

Proper tonguing can only be accomplished by using correct support.

It is Tuesday. If I'd finished the review and practised my horn, I'd be on the water on this perfectly calm morning. I'd be admiring the pod of pelicans preening on the bank, scooping into the air if I got too close. Instead, I phone my father and ask if he knows this word, adamantine. "I've heard it," he says, "but I don't know what it means." I say, "If you had one guess?" He says, "Maybe, the source of all things, like Adam, the beginning of it all?"

Dad opens his dictionary, reading aloud: "Unyielding, firm, immovable… Too hard to be cut or broken. Unbreakable. Impenetrable." He harrumphs cheerfully, says, "I was quite wrong!" I thank him, tell him about the Mozart and Haydn concert I'm playing next weekend, invite him along. He says he'll come, then asks about my wheel alignment. Reminds me to get it sorted. I say I will, as soon as I've finished the review. And after my practice. Today is the day.

It is Tuesday, and my father offers to meet me at the hospital where magnets and electrons will reveal the interior of my son's skull – may it never be cut or broken. "You don't have to, Dad," I say. "Like I said to the kid, it's too soon to panic." He says, "As a parent, what else can you say?" He says, "I'm coming; I am adamant." I say, "Thanks, but rather not." I tell my father how last time he wouldn't even allow me into the room where he lay on the stretcher to enter the doughnut-shaped machine. "If it's serious," I say, "there'll be a hard road ahead."

In "Spring Peepers, Summer Flowering" *my father and I/ share a memory of/ staying awake to witness/ the night-blooming cereus/ white queen flower/ a balm for the heart/ blooms in the backyard/ just once before withering.*

It is Tuesday, and in the waiting room my son flips open a sports magazine, shows me an article on Peter van Kets, who spent seventy-six days rowing solo across the Atlantic. "That something you would like?" I ask. "Not me," he says. "I think about it," I say. My son snorts in disgust. I point to the athlete's statement of faith: *My belief in Christ saw me through the difficult times…* and ask if he saw that. He nods and says, "Not a good enough reason." I say, "But I like the idea." He says, "Don't." I say, "Maybe I'll just row around Robben Island." He raises an eyebrow, saying nothing.

The radiographer arrives and asks the pregnant woman beside us to return for another block. She hands her the navy gown to change into and turns to us, apologising for the delay. She promises my son he's next. He says, "Thank you, ma'am." I cover my smile with my hand, knowing my pride embarrasses him. But when she leaves, he nudges me: "You never saw manners before?" I say, "Not so often as when I go out with you."

He asks for a scrap of paper to explain an equation he learned today. He crosses out, starts again. His new teacher was a Maths Olympiad, and gives his students old papers to work through in class.

My son shows me the formula: $A = \sum a_1, a_2, a_3 \tilde{O} a_n$. I say, "That a quadratic equation?" I angle the paper, holding it further away from me. I have grown long-sighted. He shakes his head, mumbling, figuring the steps aloud, holding the paper close to his face.

I never did that at school. It looks like the equations I tried in Psych III. And failed. "Is that calculus? Or stats?" He says, "Stay with me," and points again at the tiny marks he's made on the page. "You follow, Mama, okay?" I tell him I'm trying, but stats were never my strong suit. He says, "Never mind that, Mama. Just follow me now."

Acknowledgements

Earlier versions of these stories appeared in the following publications:

- The Edge of the Pot – *Per Contra*, Fall 2006
- Still Life in the Art Room – *African Compass: New Writing from Southern Africa*, Cape Town, Spearhead, 2005
- Nymph – *Touch: Stories of Contact by South African Writers*, K.M. Szczurek (ed.), Cape Town, Zebra Press, 2009
- On a Broomstick – *Bed Book of Short Stories*, Hichens, J. (ed.), Cape Town, Modjadji, 2010
- Postcards from November – *Per Contra*, Summer 2007
- Ride the Tortoise – *Chimurenga 11, Conversations with poets who refuse to speak*, N. Edjabe (ed.), Cape Town, 2007
- Signs from the Kitchen – *Temenos*, Fall 2007
- Boston Brown Bread – *Diner*, Volume 6, 2006
- The Exact Location of the Exit – *Home Away: 24 hours, 24 cities, 24 writers*, L. Greenberg (ed.), Cape Town, Zebra Press, 2010
- Tease – *Open: An erotic anthology by South African women writers*, K. Schimke (ed.), Cape Town, Oshun, 2008

The following stories are forthcoming:

- Snap – forthcoming in anthology of South African writing, 2012
- You Pay for the View – forthcoming in *Green Dragon Short Stories from SA*, Dye Hard Press, Johannesburg, 2012

My thanks go to all who offered a hand in the making of these stories, in particular to:

Dumisani Sibiya, for translation assistance.

Mary Akers, Randall Brown, Eric Bosse, Myfanwy Collins, Lydia Copeland, Katrina Denza, Pia Z. Ehrhardt, Utahna Faith, Kathy Fish, Avital Gad-Cykman, Scott Garson, Greg Gerke, Susan Henderson, Tiff Holland, Jeff Landon, Mary Miller, Darlin Neal, Jennifer Pieroni, Jim Ruland, Gail Siegel, Claudia Smith, Carrie Hoffman Spell, who welcomed the first words.

Amanda Ngozi Adichie, Ramesh Avadhani, Ann Amodeo, Jo Barris, Judith Beck, Gary Cadwallader, G.W. Cox, Lucinda Nelson Dhavan, Viet Dinh, Tricia Dower, Pamela Erens, Xujun Eberlein, Petina Gappah, Cliff Garstang, Alicia Gifford, Joseph M. Faria, T.J. Forrester, Heather Fowler, Vanessa Gebbie, Jeremy Huff, Debbie Ann Ice, Miriam Kotzin, Wenonah Lyon, Kuzhali Manickavel, Mary McCluskey, Jim Nichols, Carol Novack, Ellen Parker, Colin Pink, Marcia Lynx Qualey, Kay Sexton, Anna Sidak, Maryanne Stahl, Girija Tropp, Ania Vesenny, Binyavanga Wainana, Joan Wilking and Bonnie ZoBell, workshop companions from afar, who took my work seriously.

Erica Emdom, Christa Kuljian, Christine Lucia, Safiya Mangera, Isabella Morris, Brett Petzer, Hazel Frankel, Elizabeth Trew and Monique Verduyn, my local workshop companions who cared.

Kim Chinquee, Hugh Hodge, Estelle Jobson, Walter Mony, Pamela Nichols, G.C. Smith and Ben Williams, who nurtured my dream.

Karen Jennings, Helen Moffett, Brian Reynolds and Roy Robins, for astute reading and straight talk.

Tim Hyslop, Gail and Keith Stacey, Norman and Joy Jobson, who endured.

Glossary

bliksemed	to hit someone or something hard
fafi	betting game
Gogo	Granny
hijab	veil that covers the head, worn by some Muslim women
imali	money
joggie	attendant at a petrol station, usually a young man
kafee	café, small shop selling essentials
kikoi	sarong
kom	come on, come here
laatlammetjie	child born long after older siblings (literally, "late lamb")
makwerekwere	perjorative term for outsider, or foreigner
mbira	traditional African keyboard
mealie meal	maize meal
naartjie	citrus fruit, similar to tangerine
ntombi	girl
rondavel	round hut, usually with thatched roof
sawubona	greetings (in Zulu)
spanspek	honeydew melon
spiccato	plucking (musical term)
tjommie	pal
ukhamba	beer pot
umlungu	white person
vlei	shallow body of water, often seasonal
vrot	drunk (literally, rotten)
vuvuzela	horn, often blown at soccer matches